House of Tales

Antoine R. Marshall

Editor: Shanell N. Marshall

Cover Design: Mann Made Productions

ISBN: 979-8-89184-523-7
ISBN-13: 979-8-89184-523-7

DEDICATION

I dedicate this book to the God who his bless me with the talent to write and tell stories. I dedicate this book to all whom support, believed and should love to be and everything I've done. I dedicate this book to all who dare to dream. Those who are not afraid to go after what they want. My goal is to encourage others to go after their passion through storytelling. It is never easy pursuing your dreams. If it was many people would be doing what they love. With this book I want readers to feel as if they are in a movie. I want to take you the reader to another world through fantasy, thriller or sci-fi with real life messages. I dedicate the book to all those who do not let anything hold them back. Those who are not afraid to stand alone for the greater good. To those who do not care how silly or unpopular things look. With God there is no limit to how high and far you can go in life. I challenge you to not just dream but do. I challenge you to be consistent in everything you do. I challenge you to love yourself enough and understand you deserve the very best. You owe it to yourself. Bring your dreams to life. You have that power, so use it. Remember faith without work is dead. Lastly, I want to thank you for the love and support you have should be throughout the years.

CONTENTS

About the Book

This book is about three co-workers from a removal company who are ordered to remove items from a house thought to be abandoned. As they begin to clean and remove items, they realize that someone or something is still occupying the home. The occupant convinces them to let him tell them four stories. Fourth stories that deals with "faith, survival, life change decisions". The four stories are the following "12 Gauge" Ryan finds out that it is better to keep his mouth closed, for his words come back to corrupt his own body. "Lot Wife" Brent's family comes across a couple who seems to be the hope Brent needs. Once they leave for the valley the nightmare begins. Whatever you do not look back…for it may be the end of you. "Old Macdonald" This isn't your childhood nursery Rhyme. A school fencing team is about to find out some things are as what they seem. As the bus driver is driving, the bus ends up getting a flat tire which sparks the beginning of their terror. "Abaddon" Lori has three choices to choose from. Faith in God, do Satan's work, or stay an atheist and ignore what may or may not be real.

Jacob, India, and Larry find out after the stories end that they are the story. All stories will lead them down one path. If not careful, it will be a path of no return. "This is how the story ends".

ACKNOWLEDGMENTS

I would like to first acknowledge Jesus/God. Think you in the name of Jesus for allowing me wake up every day and put my best foot forward. I do not take any time spent on the planet for granted. I pray that my light shines through my work. I would also like to acknowledge my wife who puts up with my wild ambitions. Thank you for always being my biggest fan and support system. From helping film different projects and not knowing anything about film…yet you are always their when I need the help. You make it easy for me to go out, create and do the things I love. Lastly, I would also like to acknowledge my brother from another Mother Camden Walker. You have always been a brother to me since the day we met at ten years old. The kind words you have spoken over me do not go unnoticed. Thank you for always showing love brother. I also want to acknowledge everyone who genuinely should love me. Thank you for your endless support. Everything I do I do because I love it and it is my passion, I pray that rubs off on others.

THIS SUCKS

(**A moving crew is hired to** remove belongings from a house that is believed to be abandoned. Jacob, India, and Larry are the crew hired to move items from the house to storage. They are not too happy about doing this. It is Friday at 2:00pm based on the size of the house is going to take them to 8pm to transfer storage. They are heading to the house in a blue company van.)

Larry: This sucks man!

India: We are going to be working until eight or nine o'clock. I have a date tonight and I am going to have to reschedule.

Jacob: A date? Don't know body want to go out with you.

(Jacob and Larry both laugh.)

India: Jacob, shut your punk butt up! And Larry, I know you are not laughing. When was the last time someone should any interest in your musty butt.

Larry: Why are you coming at me? Don't get mad at me. You are the one lying about a date.

Jacob: The only date you have waiting for you is a date with your toy lightsaber and a special movie.

(Both Larry and Jacob laugh.)

India: God, you both are so lame.

Larry: Man! Why did they schedule us to remove stuff from this stupid house?

India: Right! Jacob, was this your idea?

Jacob: No, Mr. Wright said it was urgent that we get this house down today. Must be some big investors looking to buy the property soon. He said we must be the ones to knock this out.

Larry: Did he really say that, or did you volunteer because you need some money?

India: Jacob, I just know you did not volunteer us to do this job.

(India and Larry gives Jacob the side eye.)

Jacob: Okay Okay…yes, I did volunteer us.

(India and Larry gets frustrated.)

Larry: Damn man! Why didn't you come to us and ask us if we wanted to do this?

India: Jacob, you are an ass whole this.

Jacob: Aye, check it. We are getting double overtime for this.

Larry: Man! I don't care about that! It should be triple overtime.

Jacob: Look, I will make this up to you both, I promise.

(Larry and India look at each other and look at Jacob.)

Larry and India: Oh, you definitely will make this up.

(They are now pulling up to the house. The grass is tall, filled with weeds. The is big will dingy color burgundy bricks. There are cracks throughout the front of the house. As they park Larry and India stare out the window looking at the house.)

India: This is the house?

Larry: It does not look like anyone has lived here in over fifty years.

Jacob: This is definitely a creepy house. Let's get this done quickly.

India: Well, well…look who is regretting taking this job.

(They get out of the van. All three of them stand in the walkway looking at the house.)

Larry: Why does it feel like something is staring back at us?

India: Oh no, is the little baby afraid to go into the big bad house?

(Jacob and India laugh.)

Larry: Shut up! Let's get this over with.

(Jacob heads to the back of the van and opens it. They grab their equipment and proceed to the front door of the house. Jacob goes in his pocket and pulls out the key to the house. He unlocks the door and opens it. Dust kicks up in the air as the door opens. They look at each other.)

Larry: Well, which one of us is going in first?

India: God! You both are cowards.
(India bumps them as she enters. Jacob and Larry shake their heads and follow behind. There are boxes and old antiques such as lamps, statues both small and large. Old pictures, paint piling from the walls. The house has a mildew smell.)
Jacob: We need to open some of these blinds so some light can come in.
India: Who use to live here?
Jacob: I don't know. I was just told the house had been abandoned for a long time.
Larry: Dude! Look at all these antiques. A lot of these items must be worth some money. Like, look at this little statue…Wait, is this gold?
(Jacob and India take a look at the statue themselves.)
Jacob: I think this is made out of gold.
Larry: They want us to throw this out? Look at these paintings on the wall.
Jacob: Really, they want us to put these items in storage.
India: So, someone else can come and cash in on this later?
Larry: India makes a good point, which is rare.
(India gives Larry the middle finger.)
Jacob: Let's just get this house empty. I don't want to be here longer than I have to. We should split up and take different rooms to start cleaning out.
Larry: Split up! Why the hell for?
India: Here we go…Larry, you are the poster child of useless.
Larry: What? I am just saying, I think we get done faster if we are all in the same part of the house.
(Jacob laugh.)
Jacob: Come on guys. We've been here for half an hour already. We are wasting time. I would like to be done before dark if possible.
Larry: I know you are not trying to rush us. Here because your dumb butt thought this was a great idea.
Jacob: You know what? You both can stand there. I am about to get started.
(Jacob leaves the living room and heads down the hallway.)
Larry: Where are you going?
(Larry turns to India.)

Larry: Where is he going?
(India looks at Larry crazy.)
India: Um…Maybe to work.
(India heads upstairs. Larry talks to himself.)
Larry: Why are we splitting up? Dawg! These fools know nothing.
(Larry starts looking through more stuff and bagging things up. As Jacob is walking down the hall, he is checking out the pictures on the wall. The pictures look to have been taken in the 40s or 50s. A particular picture. This picture is an image of three people who looked like they were part of some trash company. All three people are dressed in uniform, almost similar to what Jacob and his team are wearing now. But the picture is in black and white with an old retro look. The first room in the hallway is just a few feet from the picture. Jacob opens the door, and a strong pungent odor hits him right in the face. He covers his face and steps back.)
Jacob: Damn! What is that smell?
(Jacob put his mask on and begins to start cleaning. India is in the first bedroom upstairs. There is old mildew clothes, papers and other debris on the floor, dresser, and desk. India is cleaning not too far from the door but face the wall which is opposite across from the bedroom door. She has her ear pods on. While she is cleaning the bedroom door across from the room, she is in door opens. Nothing is standing there. She is unaware of this. Larry is still in the living room going through everything. He sees and picks up a gold necklace with a gold pillar bar. There is a name engraved on the pillar bar "Alice".)
Larry: Ain't no way I'm putting this in storage. This must be worth a few hundred dollars.
(Larry puts the necklace in his pocket and finished scavenging through all the boxes and trash. Jacob is still in the bedroom cleaning and sorting out everything that will be trash or going to storage. He picks up some old clothes and finds a decomposing rat. It catches him off guard and he jump back.)
Jacob: What the hell man! India and Larry are right. We probably should not have taken this job.
(Behind Jacob, he hears footsteps. He turns around thinking it is Larry or India.)

Jacob: India! Larry! Is that you? India...Larry!
(No answer, but he still hears movement in the hallway. Jacob heads to the hallway.)
Jacob: Aye! I hear you guys in the hallway.
(Jacob looks in the hallway and no one is there.)
Jacob: That's weird...
(Jacob shakes his head and goes back into the room and finishes cleaning. India is cleaning and dancing to her music. As she is cleaning off the desk, she notices a crumpled piece of paper in the corner of the wall. She picks it up and unravels the paper. It reads "Don't let him tell you a story". India thinks nothing of it and throws it in the bag for trash. Larry finds a picture of an old creepy looking man sitting in a chair with kids who look like teenagers sitting around him.)
Larry: Who is this supposed to be the pied piper?
(Larry tosses the picture to the trash bag. He turns around and looks through a box next to him. Larry turns back around, and the picture is right back where he found it. He has a puzzle look on his face.)
Larry: I thought I tossed you to the trash.
(He hunches his shoulders and tosses it again in the trash. Jacob finished most of the room he is in. He heads over to the living room.)
Jacob: Hey Larry, I am going to check out the kitchen and basement.
Larry: Here you go again. You keep wandering off and messing around and disappear here. I'm leaving you.
Jacob: Whatever man. And stop taking stuff.
Larry: Aye, mind your business.
(Jacob checks out the kitchen. He opens the refrigerator and sees rotten food and spoiled milk. The smell is horrendous.)
Jacob: Man! Come on!
(Jacob slams the refrigerator door quickly. He immediately turns around to the sound of one of the kitchen chairs moving. He gets spook.)
Jacob: You know what...Larry is in my head. That's all it is.
(Jacob goes down to the basement. He flicks the switch for the lights. As Jacob is walking down the stairs, he looks up and sees words that read "The stories begin". He keeps walking

down. Once reach the bottom of the basement stairs, there is another sentence that reads "This where the stories end". He keeps looking around. In the middle of the floor lies a rocking chair. Jacob walks over to the bookshelf and sees pictures of groups of people from kids to adults sitting around an old creepy man in the rocking chair.)

Jacob: What is this place?

(Jacob calls for Larry and India.)

Jacob: Larry! India! Come check this out.

(Larry hears Jacob and heads towards him.)

Larry: Oh, he must have found something very valuable.

(Larry rubs his hands together with excitement as he is heading toward Jacob.)

Larry: Yes sir! What did you…

(Larry stops in mid-sentence.)

Larry: Jacob, what the hell is this?

Jacob: Man! I don't know. There are a lot of pictures with people sitting around this old creepy man.

(Larry takes a look at the pictures.)

Larry: Wait a minute! I've seen a similar picture upstairs with the same guy. There were five teenagers sitting on the floor around him…Jacob, what kind of cult B.S is this.

Jacob: I have no clue. Where is India?

Larry: I think she is upstairs still.

(India finds another piece of paper underneath the dresser. She reaches for it and reads it. It read "Don't let him tell the stories". This is repeated all over the paper. She finds more notice with warning on it. Something is coming. As India is focus on what she found, there is something coming up behind her. It grabs her off guard…she immediately screams, turn around and start swinging. It is Larry and Jacob.)

Larry and Jacob: Aye, India chill! Stop!

India: Ya'll scared the crap out of me! Why are ya'll sneak up on me like that?

Jacob: Girl, we've been calling your name all through the house.

Larry: Ha! You up here scared. I told you not to split up.

India: Shut up!

Jacob: What is that in your hand?

India: I'm not sure, but these notices are all through this room.

It's like someone is trying to warn from something.
Larry: Let me see this.
(India gives Larry the notices. Larry reads them and passes them to Jacob.)
Larry: Jacob, do you think these have something to do with those pictures we found.
India: What pictures?
Jacob: I don't know, but I'm sure there is some connection.
India: What pictures?
Jacob: We found some weird photos of this creepy looking old man in a rocking chair with a few people sitting around him. Looking like he is telling them a story. Each photo has a different group of people, from kids to adults.
India: What? Where? In this house?
Larry: India come check this out.
(They head back down to the basement.)
India: Did ya'll see the writing on the ceiling?
Jacob: I did.
Larry: No, I don't know how I miss that.
(India looks around.)
India: This is creepy!
(India examines the pictures. She turns around and sees the chair in the middle of the basement floor.)
India: This chair been down here the whole time too.
(Larry and Jacob are shocked.)
Jacob: That chair was not there before we came and got you.
India: what? Stop playing.
Larry: No, Jacob is right. There was no chair there.
(India gives them both the side eye.)
India: Okay, so this chair appeared in thin air. Yall playing with the wrong one. I am about to head outside and get some fresh air. This house stinks and so do you both.
(India heads up the stairs. Jacob and Larry follow behind.)
Larry: Jacob, was that chair there and we just missed it?
Jacob: Man, I could have sworn there was no chair there.
(As they take a few steps up. They hear the rocking chair rock back and forth. Both Larry and Jacob turn around. They could not believe their eyes. How could this be possible. Confusion and fear come over them both.)

Jacob: Larry, are you seeing what I'm seeing?
Larry: Yes. No way this is real what we are looking at.
(India is halfway through the house, but she wants to tell them off about the tricks both Larry and Jacob are trying to play. She heads back to the basement.)
India: Nothing, Yall both can kiss my…
(India stop in mid-sentence once she seen both Larry and Jacob standing still as if they were both frozen.)
India: What are yall doing?
(India gets close to the bottom and sees what they both see.)
India: Who is this? Where did he come from?
Jacob: We don't know. We turned around and he was there. Just sitting there rocking back and forth, staring.
India: He can't be the man from the pictures.
Larry: It is.
India: Did you talk to him?
Larry: No. I'm still trying to make since on how he got here if this house is supposed to be abandoned.
Jacob: Sir, are you okay?
(The creepy man did not answer. He just kept rocking back and forth in the chair. Jacob tries again speaking to him.)
Jacob: Hey man, listen. I don't think you are supposed to be here. Do you need some help? Is there someone we can call for you?
(Still no answer from the creepy old man. He is just rocking in the chair with a sinister smell and black eyes.)
India: Guy's lets go. We can call someone back at the office. They can tell us what we should do.
Larry: Good Idea.
(They quickly head up the basement stairs. As soon as they got to the door, the door slammed, keeping them from leaving the basement. They look at each other. Larry and Jacob both try to open the door, but it will not budge.)
India: Open the door.
Larry: What the hell do you think we are trying to do!
Jacob: Stand back!
(Jacob tries to kick the door down. He kicks three times as hard as he can. Not a scratch on the door.)
Larry: Watch out!

(Larry rams his body against the door as hard as he can twice. The door still does not budge. Larry stands back and grabs his shoulder.)

Larry: Damnit! That hurts.

(They hear laughter coming from the basement.)

Jacob: Was that…

Larry: Yeah, that fool down there laughing.

(Larry heads back down the stairs.)

India: Larry what are you about to do?

Larry: I'm about to check this punk! This is clearing a game to him.

Jacob: Yeah, he must have a remote somewhere in his pocket to use to close the door.

(They all follow Larry back down. Larry starts to go off on the creepy old man.)

Larry: Look here you little pedophile! Open this damn door now!

(Larry approaches the old man. Jacob pulls Larry back.)

Jacob: Hey man, forgive my friend. We just want to get out of here and see what's going on. Clearly you are still living here, so we will clear this up with our company.

(The old man finally moves. He looks up at Jacob.)

Old Man: Would you like to hear a story?

(The old man smiles with dark cold black eyes.)

Jacob: What?

Old Man: Would you like to hear a story?

(India remember the warnings she found.)

India: No!

(India pulls Jacob and Larry to the side.)

India: This is what all those notices was warning us about. Don't let him tell us stories.

Jacob: Okay, what do we do then? The door is locked and there are no windows to crawl out of.

(The old man speaks again.)

Old Man: It's time for a story…I'll tell you stories for your freedom.

Larry: Man! You old goat…No one wants to hear your stupid stories.

Old Man: I'll tell you stories. It will set you free.

(Larry looks to India and Jacob.)

Larry: I'm not staying down here with him...We need to figure something out fast.

Jacob: Maybe we should listen to his stories.

India: Are you dump or are you stupid? I just said we should not listen to his stories.

Jacob: Well India, what's your bright idea? I'm all ears.

Larry: I know! We can beat the crap out of him and make him open the door.

(Jacob looks at Larry crazy.)

India: I mean, that's not a bad idea. Jacob, don't go over to him.

(Jacob walks over to the old creepy man.)

India: What are you doing?

Jacob: If we listen to your stories, you will unlock the door and let us out.

(The creepy old man looks at Jacob with those cold black eyes and smiled.)

Old Man: I'll tell you stories that will set you free.

(There was something sinister about that statement, but Jacob agreed to it.)

Jacob: Okay we will listen to your stories.

(Jacob walks over to Larry and India.)

Jacob: I told him we will listen to his stories.

Larry: What?

India: You are a damn fool!

Jacob: We don't have no other option. As soon as he is done and open that door we are out of here.

India: This is such a bad I idea but let's get this over with.

(They reluctantly walk over to him.)

Larry: Alright man, let's get started.

Old Man: Please sit.

Larry: Hell naw! Just talk.

Old Man: Please sit.

(They look at each other. Jacob sits first slowly. India and Larry followed slowly after Jacob. The old man stops rocking in the chair. He leans forward with his eyes closed, smelled and taste the air in front of them. India frauds.)

India: What are you doing?

(He opens his eyes with smile and look down at them.)
Old Man: Shall we begin.
Jacob: Man come! Enough with the games!
Old Man: Eagerness. I like it. This just story is a story you can appreciate Larry…I call this first story "12 gauge". The power of the tongue.

12 Guage

(Ryan is sitting in the parking lot with two friends. They are talking about their boss and how unfair he is.)

Toine: Man! I can't stand our boss!

Ryan: I know right! This fool doesn't care about anything.

Chase: This man needs to get laid or something.

Toine: Please. No one wants him.

(Toine shakes his head.)

Ryan: I know one thing. Mr. Walker needs to lay off me. Every time I come in; he got something to say.

Chase: Right! He needs a day off. Shoot he can go pay for sex.

(They all laugh.)

Ryan: I wish he would fall down a flight of stairs and break his neck.

(While wishing this, a shooting star flies over his head at the same time.)

Chase: Dang bro. That's harsh…but I feel you.

Toine: Alright guys, I'm about to take off.

Ryan: Yeah, me too.

Chase: Aye, we not hanging tonight?

Ryan: Bro, you never want to go home.

Chase: And set with my grandmother…man, I am about to get into a little something tonight.

(Ryan and Toine laughs and shoot him off. Everyone leaves and goes their separate ways.)

(Next day Ryan wakes up stretches and goes through his normal morning routine. While getting himself together, he stops at the mirror and sees a rash on his neck. It looks kind of like scales. He doesn't think much of it.)

(Ryan heads to work. As he walks into work, both these friends come running to him.)

Toine: Ryan, did you hear?
Ryan: Hear what?
Toine: Mr. Walker is dead!
Ryan: What?! What do you mean?
Chase: He's dead man! Mr. Walker is Dead!
Ryan: How? What happened?
Chase: Mr. Walker fell down the stairs and broke his neck.
(As his friends are talking about that happened, Ryan had a puzzled look on his face. The new manger calls everyone to the back, to discuss what happened to Mr. Walker.)
New Manger: Hey, guys. I know we are all shocked about what happened. It was a freak accident. If anyone needs to talk, we will have grieving counselors here. Other than that, let's all do our best today to get through this day.
(Everyone goes back to work after the new manager dismisses.)
(Ryan leaves work with friends. As they are walking to the parking lot, a homeless man walks by harassing them. They tried to shoot him away.)
Homeless man: Hey hey..fellas let me hold some change.
Toine: Sorry sir, we don't have anything.
Homeless man: Aw, brothers come on. Ya'll got something on you.
Chase: Man! We broke too.
Homeless man: Oh, so you boys are homeless too.
(Homeless man laughs.)
Ryan: Aye. Move on man. We don't have time for your bull.
Homeless man: You don't have to be rude.
Toine: You stink. Watch out man.
Homeless man: Your mom likes my smell…
(Homeless man laughs.)
(Toine checks the homeless man.)
Toine: What? What did you say?
(Ryan grabs Toine.)
Ryan: Toine, come on bro. Don't even sweat him.
Homeless man: Come on.
(Homeless man laughs.)
Ryan: Why don't you get hit by a car.
(Ryan's friends laugh.)

(They walk off and homeless man is still running his mouth.)

Look Out

(Some Minutes went by. Homeless man is walking towards the corn of a busy street. But there are hardly any cars coming. Suddenly, not far away there is a car coming with a female driver. As he begins to walk across, the young lady is driving and is not paying attention. She is texting, music loud, reaching down to the car floor picking things up.)

(Homeless man is crossing the street at the same time while this is going on. There is a creepy whisper in the air. As the homeless man is walking closer to the middle of the road. The car is getting closer and closer.)

(He is now in the middle of the road. The girl is closer and looks up too late. She hits him. She screams. Man, fly's and instantly dies.)

(It is now morning. Ryan wakes up and does his normal routine. Ryan sees another rash on the other side of his neck.)

Ryan: What is this? Did I get bitten by something?

(Ryan shrugs it off and heads out. Ryan is driving and sees his ex-girl walking.)

Ryan: I hope she catches AIDs.

(Ryan says this with a bitter undertone.)

(Ryan meets up with friends.)

Chase: Dawg, what happened to your neck?

Toine: Yeah, what girl was sucking on your neck?

Ryan: Shut up! I'm not sure. Maybe an allergic reaction.

(Both Toine and Chase laugh at Ryan.)

Toine: Yeah right.

Chase: Aye, yall remember that homeless man from last night?

Ryan: What about him?

Chase: Dude was hit by a car last night. He died instantly on impact.

Toine: Wow, Ryan what a coincidence right.

Chase: Bro, you killed him!

(Friends laughs.)

Ryan: That's not funny!

Chase: My bad bro, I'm just pulling your leg.
(Ryan turns around and says dang underneath his breath.)
Face to Face

(It is now night. Ryan is heading back home. Ryan gets ready for bed; he can't help but think about what happened as he lay there. It is now morning. Ryan gets up and does his normal routine.)

(Ryan gets ready for work. He notices that his right arm looks scaley and peeling. His right shoulder up to his neck was scaley and more rashes appeared.)

Ryan: What the hell is this?!

(Ryan tries to pull off the scales. He calls his doctor to make an appointment.)

(Ryan leaves out and stops at a local store for skin cream until he makes it to the doctor's office. While in the store he runs into his ex-girlfriend in the store.)

(She's wearing a large hoodie and seems to be looking for medicine too. He sees her and tries to avoid her. As he walks around the shelves, she appears right in front of him.)

(She has blemishes all over her face, neck and even hands. She was coughing a lot too.)

(In a soft creep raspy voice.)

Ruth: Hi.

Ryan: What's up? What happened to you?

(She smiles.)

Ruth: I messed up.

Ryan: What do you mean?

Ruth: Not that you really care Ryan…but I'm very sick. I thought I was being careful. Maybe I had it for a while.

Ryan: Had what?

(Ruth looks down.)

Ruth: I…I have…I have aids.

(Ryan takes two steps back in shock.)

Ryan: When and for how long have you had this?

Ruth: I do not know.

Ryan: Why do you think you get it from?

Ruth: Please. You seeing me like this brings you joy.

Ryan: Why would you say that? I would not wish…

(At that moment, Ryan remembers what he said a few days ago. He pauses and then finishes his sentence.)

Ryan: I would not wish this on anyone.

Ryan: This can't be a coincidence.

(Whispers.)

Ruth: What's a coincidence?

Ryan: Nothing. I'm sorry this happened to you.

Ruth: I guess I got what I deserved…Right?

(She laughs as he walks away. She repeats it again.)

Ruth: I guess I got what I deserved right?

(Ryan runs out of the store.)

(Ryan is now at the doctor's office. Doctor examines him.)

Doctor: So, Ryan I could not find anything major. It seems to just be an allergic reaction…Here take this and you should be good in a few days.

Ryan: What could I be allergic to?

Ryan: I never had an issue with anything.

Doctor: Ryan, sometimes we get things later in life. Our bodies go through changes often during our lifetime.

Ryan: Yeah, but this doesn't seem right. Every time I wake up there is a new rash…what kind of allergic reaction makes my skin look like this?

Doctor: I am going to be honest with you. I do not know what is causing this. It can be something you ate, mixed with stress.

Doctor: I tell you what. Let me take some blood work and I will let you know what I find.

Ryan: Yes, and please let me know soon doc.

Doctor: Until then, take some Benadryl cream and rub it on your skin.

Could it be me.

(Ryan is driving. Another driver cuts him off. Ryan yells at the driver.)

Ryan: I hope you have a heart attack.

(Suddenly Ryan sees in his rear-view mirror the car cash. Ryan stops and runs over to see what happened. Guy in car is having a heart attack.)

Ryan: Aye! Man are you okay?

(Man is struggling to breath. Holding his chest…he looks over at Ryan and tries to speak but end up dying.)

(Ryan calls 9-1-1.)

Ryan: Hello! Yes. This man crashed from having a heart attack.

Operator: Is he responsive?

Ryan: No. He's not breathing.

Operator: What's your location?

(Ryan: A dress will be added later...leading up to production.)

Operator: Okay, stay with him if you can. Sending someone now.

(As Ryan is waiting for the ambulance to arrive. There is a whisper in the background. A whisper with the wind. Ryan gets this weird feeling. Ryan looks over at the guy. His eyes were close at first…but once Ryan look over at him and was spooked to find his eyes where open.)

(Ryan runs back to his car and drives off. Ryan heads over to one of his friends' house. Walks into Toine's house.)

Ryan: Bro! Something weird is going on.

Toine: What do you mean? What happened to your skin?

Ryan: I have an allergic reaction or something.

Toine: Dawg, what kind of reaction makes your skin look like reptile skin?

Ryan: I don't know…But that's not what's important. Something is happening.

Toine: Like what?

Ryan: It seems like when I say something it happens, at least something negative.

Toine: What?! Shut up. Old goofy ass.

Ryan: Dawg! I'm telling you man. That is how it seems.

Toine: Ryan, you must be high.

Toine: I tell you what, let's test this theory out.

Ryan: How?

Toine: Well, you said when you say something negative, it happens right?

Ryan: I mean, yeah, I guess.

Ryan: But how will we test this theory?

Toine: Say something about me and let's see what happens.

Ryan: Why would I want to do that?
Toine: Right! Stupid idea…not going to let you kill me.
(Toine jokes.)
Ryan: Man! This is serious.
Toine: Okay, I got it!
Toine: What about old bitter Fred from work?
Toine: He is always angry.
Toine: Tomorrow when we go in, wish for something, or wave your magic wand.
Ryan: you got jokes I see.
Toine: Ha! Bro you will see that it is all just a coincidence.
Ryan: Alright man. I'm about to head home and relax.
Toine: And you need to rip off your skin too. Walk into my house looking like reptile from Mortal Kombat.
(They both laugh.)

The Test

Testing can be dangerous. Don't play with fire.
(Ryan is getting ready for bed. He rubs the cream on the areas that are affected on his body.)
(Ryan wakes up and goes through his normal routine. Look into the mirror. Now his whole neck and left upper arm has rashes and scales.)
Ryan: There is no way this is an allergic reaction.
(Ryan tries again to pull off some of it. He also checks his back and sees it is all rashes and scales.)
(Ryan calls his doctor's office.)
Doctor: Hello.
Ryan: Doctor. It is getting worse…This cannot be just an allergic reaction.
Doctor: Okay, your blood work will be here this afternoon.
Doctor: Don't mess with it. Keep adding cream on it…Just set tight. I will call you soon with answers and what to do next.
Ryan: Okay.
(Ryan hangs up and looks for clothes that will cover all the rashes on his body.)
(Ryan heads into work. Toine and Chase run up to Ryan smiling.)
Chase: Let's see how your superpowers work.

Ryan: So, we got jokes aye!
Toine: Look man…you a funny guy.
Ryan: I am going through stuff and ya'll cracking jokes.
Chase: Ah fool. Stop your whining.
(Ryan waves them off.)
Toine: There goes Bitter Fred.
(They both look. Chase smiles.)
Chase: So, what are you going to wish for?
Toine: Oh, I now…Have a piano fall on his head.
Chase: No. Make him explode.
Ryan: Man! Ya'll is sick!
Chase: Well, what will it be then?
(Ryan is starting to believe that there is some truth about what he is saying. He Pauses for a minute. That creepy whisper plays in the background again, as Ryan daydreams staring at Fred.)
Toine: Aye! Wake up!
(Ryan jumps a little.)
Ryan: Okay, okay…I hope Fred breaks his arm and leg.
(They are now staring at Fred waiting for something to happen. As they gaze deeper and deeper. Their manager walks up behind them and scares them.)
Manager: What are you guys doing?
(All three say nothing.)
Manager: Well can ya'll stop doing nothing, and do something like work?
Ryan: Yeah, my bad.
(Manager walks off.)
Toine: I told you fool!
Toine: It is all just a coincidence.
Chase: Right! And that stuff growing on you probably came from that girl you were missing with a few weeks back.
Ryan: Whatever man!
(Ryan turns around and takes a deep breath. He felt silly to think that he was the cause of bad things that had happened.)
(Everyone is working, and a few minutes goes by. Suddenly a loud scream came from the back room. Everyone stops and looks. One of the workers came running from the back screaming.)

Worker: Help! Help!
Manager: What happened!
Worker: Fred…He…He, broke his arm and leg!
Manager: What? How?!
Worker: He was just walking…next thing I know he start scream and he was on the ground.
(Toine and Chase look at each other and then look at Ryan. Ryan had a look of shock on his face.)
Ryan: This can't be real.
(Manager rushed over to call 9-1-1.)
Toine: Ryan, how is this possible?
Ryan: I do not know…I wish I…
(Toine stops him in mid-sentence.)
Toine: Don't even finish that sentence.
Chase: Man! I think you need to see a pastor or something. Have an exorcist done.
Tonie: Chase!
Chase: What? He literally wishes harm to anyone.
Toine: Chase is right Ryan. When did this start happening?
(Fear is all over Ryan's face as everyone else is getting Fred some help. Ryan begins to walk towards the door.)
Chase: Ryan, where you are going!
Ryan: I…I …I got to go.
(Ryan runs out. Toine calls to him as he runs out.)
Toine: Ryan! Ryan!
(Ryan runs to his car. He gets in. Ryan notices two knots that have grown on his forehead. His nails grew longer and sharp. He screams.)
Ryan: What the hell!
Ryan: What is happening to me!
(Both Chase and Toine caught up to Ryan and knocked on the door. Ryan turns around…as he turns around, they immediately jumped back.)
Chase: Ryan is that you!
(Ryan quickly turned back around to hide his face. Ryan did not answer. He quickly pulled off.)
Chase: What is going on Toine?
Toine: Man! I have no clue…but something is wrong.
Chase: Did you see his face?

Chase: Like, we were just looking at him in the shop and his face was fine.
Toine: Yeah, now he looks like some type of monster.

Death of the Tongue
Your tongue will be the death of you.
(Ryan pulls up to a local church. He looks in his back seat and grabs his hoodie to help cover his head. Ryan gets out and knocks on the door.)
(A pastor comes to the door.)
Pastor Ray: Good afternoon, how can I help you?
(Ryan head is down. He does not want to show his face. He answered with a raspy voice.)
Ryan: Pastor…Pastor.
Ryan: Something is wrong with me.
Pastor Ryan: What is it?
Pastor Ray: Do you need a hospital?
Ryan: No…No hospital can help me.
Pastor Ray: Why don't you come in.
Pastor Ray: Oh, I did not catch your name.
(Ryan slightly looks up.)
Ryan: I Ryan.
Pastor Ray: Nice to meet you, Ryan.
(Pastor Ray reach out to shake hand. Ryan shakes his hand. Pastor looks at his hand and is puzzled by what he sees. Ryan hand nails are long and sharp and rough like reptile skin.)
Pastor Ray: Come, come sit with me.
(They walk over to some seats.)
Pastor Ray: What's going on Ryan?
Ryan: Pastor, I'm not sure.
Ryan: It is like I am changing into something…Something ungodly.
Pastor Ray: When did the changings start? And how did this happen?
Ryan: It started a few days ago. I woke up one morning and my neck and arm had rashes.
Ryan: I did not think much of it at first…but each morning I woke up, things got worse.
Pastor Ray: The night before the morning, did anything take

place?

Ryan: I was just in the parking lot with friends talking about nothing.

Pastor Ray: So, nothing happened?

Pastor Ray: You did not feel sick?

Ryan: No.

Pastor Ray: May I ask what you guys was talking about?

Ryan: We was just talking trash…We also talk about our boss.

Pastor Ray: Where is your boss now?

Ryan: He died.

Pastor Ray: Sorry to hear that.

Pastor Ray: When did he die?

Ryan: That night.

Pastor Ray: You said you was talking about him. What did you say?

(Ryan paused. He thought about it. It hit him like a ton of bricks. He realizes that every time he speaks anything negative it happens.)

Ryan: We were talking about how unfair he is. We laugh and crack jokes about him.

Ryan: Then I said I hope he falls down a flight of stairs and breaks his neck. Next morning, I got to work and found out it happened.

Pastor Ray: How often have you said something negative action and it happened?

Ryan: Every time I say something like that about someone, it happens.

Ryan: It's like someone cursed me.

(Pastor Ray looks up and say I hear you lord.)

Pastor Ray: Proverbs 18:21

Ryan: What?

Pastor Ray: Proverbs 18:21 The tongue can bring death or life those who love to talk will reap the consequences.

Ryan: And what is that supposed to mean?

Pastor Ray: Our mouth is like a weapon. It is a 12-gauge shotgun.

Pastor Ray: Unfortunately, when we aim it at someone…it usually backfires. Meaning that in the process of trying to hurt someone else, we end up hurting ourselves. Sometimes it backfires later in life and sometimes it backfires immediately.

Ryan: Pastor, I don't understand.

Pastor Ray: James 3:6

And among all the parts of the body, the tongue is a flame of fire. It is a whole world of wickedness, corrupting your entire body. It can set your whole life on fire, for it is set on fire by hell itself.

(Ryan looks at his hands.)

Ryan: So, God did this to me!

Pastor Ray: No. God does not cause hurt, or does he allow pain or evil things too happened to anyone. We are the cause of our own demise.

Ryan: So, how do I fix this?

Pastor Ray: That's a conversation between you and God.

(Ryan gets mad. Jumps up.)

Ryan: Pastor! That's not an answer!

Pastor Ray: That's the only answer I can give you. The one with the answer is up there.

(Ryan stands up and began to leave)

Pastor Ray: Seek him, Ryan.

Ryan: If God cares so much, he would not have let this happened.

Pastor Ray: God did not do this Ryan.

Ryan: Oh, so I did this to myself pastor?

(Ryan walks out. Pastor Ryan yells to him.)

Pastor Ray: Seek him Ryan...You must seek him.

Seek Him

(Ryan is now walking down the street angry. Talking to himself.)

Ryan: Why have you allowed this to happen to me.

(Ryan walks past a window. He looks at it, and he does not recognize what he sees anymore. He touches the window and falls to his knees.)

(Gets up and walks through an alley. He stops and lays on the ground. Whispers follow like the wind around him. He looks around to see where this is coming from. He speaks but does not recognize the voice that comes from him.)

Ryan: Who's there?

Ryan: My…my voice.

(Ryan touches his throat. Ryan voice is deep and dark sounding.)

(A group of kids passing by on skateboards. They see Ryan and stop to see if he is okay.)

Kids: Sir! Hey…are you okay?

(Ryan turns around and screams at them to go away.)

Ryan: Leave me alone!!

(One of the kids falls back.)

Kids: What the hell man!

Kids: What are you!

Kids: He's a damn troll…Literally a troll.

(Kids take off running.)

(Ryan sets back down, folds arms and rock back and forth. He slowly looks up and sees this grim reaper figure standing there. Ryan stands up with a shock look on his face.)

(Ryan starts walking away fast…he turns around and it's gone. Ryan turns back around, and his old boss is standing there reach out to him.)

Ryan: Mr. Walker!

Ryan: Wait! You died…how are you here?

Mr. Walker: Come with us Ryan.

(Mr. Walker tries to grab him. Ryan broke loose.)

Ryan: Let me go!

(Ryan tries to run off and there is his ex-girlfriend.)

Ex-girlfriend: Ryan, come with us.

(She grabs Ryan and tries to bite him. Ryan screams.)

Ryan: Get the hell off me!

(The homeless man appears and grabs him and bites him.)

(Ryan screams in pain.)

(Next the man from the car crash and co-worker appeared too. All chatting come with us.)

Ghouls: Come with us…Come with us…Come with us.

(Ryan falls to the ground as they pull and bite at him.)

Ryan: I'm sorry…Please…I'm sorry!

Ryan: No! Please…No!

A Dream

It was all a dream.

(Ryan wakes up and finds himself in the lounge area at work. Ryan woke up sweating. He looks around with a confused look on his face.)

(He jumps up and runs to the mirror and sees that he looks normal. Ryan laughs in disbelief.)

Ryan: God that felt so real.

Chase: Aye bro. You ready? We are about to lock up and head out.

Chase: Man. Why do it look like you seen a ghost?

Ryan: Man! I have the dumbest dream ever…Like, it felt real.

Chase: Well, it looks like you had one of those wet dreams…They can feel real.

Ryan: Shut up!

(Chase laughs.)

(As Ryan heads to the car where his friends are, he felt déjà vu.)

(Ryan listens to his friends and realizes they are saying the same thing word from word, from his nightmare.)

Toine: Man! I can't stand our boss!

Chase: This man needs to get laid or something.

Toine: Please. No one wants him.

Chase: Right! He needs a day off. Shoot he can go pay for sex.

Toine: Ryan, you good bro?

Chase: Yeah, you always got something funny to say.

(Ryan has a daydreaming look on his face.)

Toine: Hello…Earth to retard.

Chase: Toine, you can't say retard no more.

Toine: Why not?

Chase: I don't know man…world is going soft, I guess.

Toine: Ryan!

Ryan: What…Oh my bad bro.

Toine: You good?

Ryan: Yes…I just had déjà vu.

Ryan: We should pray for Mr. Walker.

(Chase and Toine look at each other and laugh.)

Toine: Man. What are you on?

Ryan: I'm just saying. Maybe he's dealing with some stuff personally.

Chase: This man took a nap and woke up Dr. Martin Luther King.

Toine: Right.

(Ryan laughs.)

Ryan: Whatever dawg. I'm about to head out. I'll catch up to ya'll tomorrow.

(As Ryan gets in the car, he sees the homeless man coming over. Before the homeless man say anything, Ryan pulls out three dollars.)

Ryan: Here you go. This is all I have on me.

Homeless man: Thank you young blood. God bless you.

(Homeless man walks off. Ryan hops into the car and pulls off. Ryan phone rings and it is his ex-girlfriend.)

Ryan: Hello?

Ex-girlfriend: Hey.

Ryan: Hey.

Ex-girlfriend: Is this a bad time?

Ryan: No... it's not. I'm just leaving work.

Ex-girlfriend: Okay, cool. I was just thinking about you and thought I should give you a call.

(Ryan smiles.)

(Larry and India look at each other exhaustion. Jacob seems to be into the old man's story.)

Jacob: That was an interesting story.

Larry: Yeah, that was cool. How many more do we have to listen too?

(Old man starts rocking back and forth in the chair.)

Old Man: You'll are all most ready.

India: This is stupid. Jacob, you really into this?

Jacob: What? No, it was just an interesting story.

Old Man: This next story is fitting for you India.

India: I don't care nothing about your damn stories. I just want you to hurry up. No more pausing.

Larry: Yeah, and what you are doing is against the law. You better let us go when you are done.

(India and Larry looks over to Jacob. India nudges Jacob.)

Jacob: What what?

India: Snap out of it! I know you are not being entertained by him.

Jacob: What? No, of course not.

Old Man: Ready for the next story?

India: I said hurry up…no more breaks too!

Old Man: As you wish. I call this next story "Lot Wife". Having someone around who doesn't listen can be fatal.

Lot Wife

(Kamala and Karine pulls up to the house party. They see other classmates going in. It's their last year of high school and it will be the last time they will see many of their classmates. Kamala sees a guy she likes walking in.)

Karine: Girl, look at you.

Kamala: What?

Karine: Kamala, you sitting here blushing watching Trey walk in.

(Kamala smiles.)

Kamala: I wasn't even looking at him.

Karine: Whatever.

(They both laugh.)

Karine: But girl come on. Why are we just sitting here.

Kamala: My bad. Let's go.

(They get out of the car and head to the house. Karine gets real hype as they walk in.)

Karine: This is our last year baby! College life, sexy college boys and lots of spring break parties, here we come!

Kamala: Karine, you are crazy! But you ain't lying.

(Music playing, kids partying, everyone is chanting class 24. It echoes through the whole house. Half an hour into the party kamala is standing by the window dancing and singing with some of her other friends. While dancing she sees a girl outside on the phone. Kamala doesn't pay it no mine and keeps interacting with her friends. She turns around back towards the window and sees the girl facing the opposite direction staring straight ahead. The girl's phone is in the grass by her feet. Kamala gets closer to the window to see what she is looking at. Everyone else is oblivious to what's going on. The girl looks to frozen in place. Karine walks up behind Kamala and taps her on the shoulder.)

Karine: Hey girl.

(Kamala jumps.)
Kamala: Man! You scared me.
Karine: What are you looking at?
Kamala: This girl out there.
Karine: What girl? I don't see anyone.
(Kamala looks again and the girl is gone.)
Kamala: It was definitely a girl standing out there being weird.

Karine: Guess what? Who cares Kamala, there go Trey. Go over there and say something.
Kamala: I see him. Say what?
Karine: I don't know. Stop being lame!
Kamala: Shut up…you lame.
(Katine grabs Kamala arm and drag her over to Trey.)
Kamala: Girl wait, hold up.
Karine: Nope, let's go. If you don't do it now, you will never do it.
(She pushes kamala right in front of Trey and walks off.)
Kamala: I'm so sorry. My friend is a little off.
(Trey laughs.)
Trey: So, are you enjoying yourself.
Kamala: Yeah, it's cool.
(Both are silent for a few seconds. Kamala doesn't know what to say. Suddenly, she becomes shy. Trey looks around. Kamala looks to the side.)
Trey: Any plans after high school.
(Kamala is space out.)
Kamala: I'm sorry what?
Trey: I said, any plans after high school?
Kalama: Oh yes. Definitely college, you?
Trey: Yeah, same here. I'm going to FAMU.
(Kamala eyes lights up.)
Kamala: Really? Me too!
Trey: Yeah right.
Kamala: No, for real. I'll be studying Journalism.
Trey: That's wild. Okay, we definitely going to have to link up a few times and help each other to get through our freshman year.

(Kamala blushes.)

Kamala: Yes, that will be great.

Trey: So, any plans for prom?

(Before Kamala could answer they hear someone screaming from the back.)

Kamala: Did you hear that?

Trey: Yes, it sounds like someone screaming.

(More screams occur. The DJ turns the music off. Everyone inside the house hears their classmates outside screaming. A few go see what is going on. Some of the kids from outside ran to the back door to get back in. Screaming help. Bodies are being tossed around. A boy runs into the house with one of his arms ripped off. Screaming "It told me to turn around". The boy dies from loss of blood. Everyone in the house starts to panic. Kamala runs and search for Karine.)

Kamala: Karine! Karine!

(Everyone is running trying to hide a few goes outside. Kamala sees Karine outside in the front. She runs after her and calls her name.)

Kamala: Karine!

(Karine turns around.)

Karine: Kamala!

(At the moment that Karine turns around to run towards Kamala, she freezes. Fear begins to consume her.)

Kamala: Karine! What's wrong?

(Karine screams. Something lefts Karine into the air and breaks her neck. Kamala falls back and screams. She crawls a few feet backwards. Everything seems to move in slow motion. Many of her classmates are dead or injured. Screams begin to echo throughout the neighborhood. Karine gets up. Right at that moment she is about to turn around, Trey runs up behind her and stops her.)

Trey: Don't turn around.

Kamala: What? Why?

Trey: Everyone who turned around dies.

Kamala: What do we do then?

Trey: We must keep moving forward. To turn back is to die.

Kamala: Do you hear that?

Trey: Yes, that's how they get you. We need to leave now.

Kamala: My car is over there. We can make it.
(They run to the car. Both do their best not to look back. Trey rips the rearview mirror off. They look at each other and then look forward and drive off.)

We need to Hide.
(It is dust. Two brothers are running for cover.)
Jay: Let's go!! We need to go now! They are coming.
Louis: I'm coming!
Jay: Louis…Just leave it.
(They hear a roar in the winds. Shadows circle the house. The terror is thick in the air.)
Jay: Louis…you did not look back, did you?
(Brent looks at Jay with a scared look on his face.)
Jay: Louis, did you look back…
Brent: They kept calling me…They called to me.
Jay: NO!! Louis!
(Roaring sound returns. They both look out the window. Next, they hear something in the house upstairs.)
(Jay and Louis look at each other. Ran out of the house.)
Jay: Louis! Don't look back.
Louis: Put…put I they are coming for me…
(The ghouls grab Louis. Jay tries to fight them off. Brent screams.)
Louis: Jay!!!! Help…. help….
(Louis screams in pain and fear.)
(Jay tries to run. He falls and gets dragged off by his feet. Screams echo.)
(A couple hears the screams. They go to check it out and see nothing. Then as soon as they return around the women throat get slash. Her boyfriend screams as she falls into his arms. He looks up and his eyes turn cloudy white. Then slash across his face.)
(You can hear screams throughout the city.)

Home is where the heart is.

(Brent is ready to leave for the valley and believes he and his family need to leave immediately.)

Brent: Natasha, we need to leave today. We will be safe in the valley.

(Natasha looks disgusted at Brent.)

Natasha: Who told you we will be safe there? And how do you know it even exists?

Brent: Something inside of me is telling us to go and to go soon.

Natasha: Something inside of you? Really?!

Brent: Yes, and I feel that we need to act on this, or we will not survive.

(Natasha rolls eyes.)

Brent: What is wrong with you? You heard about the deaths and disappearance that's been running rampant around us. What other proof do you need?

Natasha: I do not believe that danger or some darkness is coming. I mean Brent, look around you. Our friends and family are partying and living good. None of them are worried or scared. Yet, you have some voice in your head or stomach telling you to flee all that we know and love.

(Brent has a sad look on his face.)

Brent: Natasha, I know you are scared, and I know this is hard. Trust me! I do not want to leave anyone either, but something is telling me to run.

Brent: You know their mindset and values. That's why they are doing what they are doing.

Natasha: What is their mindset, Brent? Hm…

Natasha: Since something is telling you to leave so badly, maybe you should just go by yourself. Like, why no one else is having that same feeling you have?

(Brent looks at Natasha sideways.)

Brent: I do not understand why you are acting like this, but I am not leaving my kids. People are dying left and right of us, and that does not bother you. You would rather party and act crazy instead of protecting your family.

(Natasha looks furious.)

Natasha: That's right Brent! You are such a goodie two

shoes! I'm the heathen…the bad guy, right?
Brent: That's not what I'm saying or believe!
Natasha: Yeah Yeah! We know what you believe Brent.
Brent: Since when did you have a problem with what I believe in? I don't even recognize this person you are right now.
Natasha: Boy, please! I'm sick of your righteous butt!
Brent: What?!
Kids: Stop fighting!!
Brent: Now look! You are scaring the kids!
Natasha: I'm scaring the kids?! NO! You are scaring the kids with your nonsense.
(Brent calls kids over to him and hugs them both)
Brent: Kids, I am so sorry. I love you both and things will get better. I promise you.
Kids: It's okay dad. We love you too.
(Natasha folds arms and looks angry.)
(A knock at the door. Brent and Natasha look up and Brent looks frighten)
Natasha: Who is it?

Who is it?
(Brent opens the door and sees a couple standing there.)
Brent: Hi, can I help you?
(Couple looks at each other and smiles.)
Jason: I'm Jason and this is my wife, Mia. We are passing by heading to the valley.
(Brent face lights up.)
Mia: Can we come in?
Natasha: Don't let them in! We do not know them. What if they try to harm us?
(Brent turns to Natasha.)
Brent: Oh, now you are worried?
(Brent shakes his head.)
Jason: I promise we mean you know harm. We just want to rest for a second and then we are gone.
(Brent steps to the side.)
Brent: Yes, please come in.
Mia: Thank you!

(Couple comes in and sits down. Mia looks at kids and smile.)

Mia: Hi.

(Kids have a shy look on their face.)

Kids: Holla.

Mia: Your family is beautiful.

Natasha: Hm.

Brent: Thank you!

(Jason is looking out of the window.)

Jason: Have you guys been out there lately?

Brent: No, not the past two days. How bad is it?

Jason: It's a nightmare. It is like we are in a horror movie. The darkness comes and rips your soul from you. Those who go out and look back die.

Natasha: I don't believe it.

Mia: Believe it! We've seen the horrors. No one knows where it comes from or why it's here.

(Natasha gets up.)

Natasha: So, how did you guys hear about the valley? Let me guess…You had a gut feeling.

(Both Jason and Mia look at each other.)

Jason: Yes, that is exactly what it was. So loud as if someone was right in front of us telling us to go.

Mia: Natasha, did you have the same feeling.

Natasha: Um…No.

Natasha: Come on guys. Enough of this fairytale BS. Like really?! This will blow over. Some many people are doing fine. It is a little cold. Nothing more, nothing less.

Brent: Natasha! Enough!

Mia: No, it's okay. Most people can only believe what they can see. Even when many see it, they still won't believe it. That's just how faith works.

Natasha: So, why is it only you three who have this feeling?

Jason: We cannot explain it. We just know what we need to do.

Brent: Guys, please excuse my wife. She is…

Natasha: I'm what?!

Brent: Never mind.

(Both Jason and Natasha look sad at what they are hearing

from Natasha.)
(Natasha leaves the room.)
(Mia walks over to the kids.)
Kid 1: Have you been to the valley?
Mia: No. I haven't.
Kid 2: How do you know it is safe.
Mia: I do not know. But what I do know is that my faith has never let me down.
Kid 1: Where are your kids?
Mia: We don't have any.
(Jason walks over to them and puts his hands on Mia Shoulder.)
Jason: It just isn't our time yet…but we will be blessed with a child soon one day.
(Mia looks up at Jason.)
Mia: Jason, we should be leaving soon.
Jason: Yes, you are right.
Brent: Wait, hold up! Maybe we can all go together. The more the stronger right?
Jason: You know what? You are right, Brent. We can work together. But the walk is long.
Brent: That is no problem. I have a car that we can all fit in and get close to the valley as possible.
(Natasha comes back into the room.)
Natasha: So, we are really doing this?

(Brent pulls Natasha to the side.)
Natasha: What?
Brent: Natasha, please trust me on this.
Natasha: I'm going too, aren't I? So, let's go. I just want to see your faces when you realize this was all for nothing.

Time to go.

(As everyone is getting ready, they hear a loud scream coming from outside. They pause and look at each other. Brent turns to his kids and walks over to comfort them.)
Kid 1: Dad who was that?
Brent: I'm not sure.

(They hear another scream from a different person.)

(Jason looks on.)

Jason: It's here…We need to move now!

Natasha: I'm sure there is some explanation for what we just heard.

(Mai is now getting a little annoyed with Natasha's bitterness.)

Mia: I am not sticking around to find out.

Brent: Hurry! Only grab what you can carry.

(Everyone is scrambling around to grab what they need.)

Brent: The car is just a few feet away.

Jason: Great! Remember when we head out…do not look back for any reason.

Natasha: Come on man! Really Brent?

Mai: Natasha, we will survive better if we are all working together.

Natasha: Whatever!

(Jason opens the door. They hear more cries for help.)

Brent: Everyone is ready?

(Everyone nods their heads.)

Brent: Okay, let's go!

(Everyone runs out the house to the car and quickly gets in. Suddenly, they hear growling and a raspy voice sound behind them. They want to look back.)

Jason: Remember! No matter what you hear do not look back!

(Brent tries to start the car.)

Brent: What the Heck!

Jason: What is it?

Brent: The car won't start.

Jason: Wait. Pop the hood. I can check it.

Mia: No! You cannot go out there.

Jason: I'll be quick.

(Jason grabs his jacket and holds it over his head to keep him from looking back. He opens the hood and jiggles the battery. Now the car has started.)

Mia: Jason! Hurry up!

(Jason gets back into the car. They pull off.)

We have arrived.

(Brents car gets them close before the car stops, but they still must make it to the valley which is now about two miles away.)

Brent: Oh no!

Natasha: Now what?

Brent: The car. It's dead now.

(Whisper in the air telling Jason to turn around. It is okay…we are your friend.)

(Another whisper sounds like Jason's mother.)

Mother of Jason: Jason, it's me…your mother. Help me.

Jason: Shut up! You are not my mother.

(Jason ignores the whisper and avoids looking back.)

Jason: That's okay! We are less than two miles away.

Mia: Can we make it?

Jason: Yes, our faith got us this far. Cannot give up now.

Jason: Remember do not look back.

(Everyone gets out of the car and starts walking.)

Kid 2: Dad, it's hard not to look back.

(Brent brings kid 2 closer to him.)

Brent: I know sweetheart, but we must. We are almost there.

(The wind blows, yet within the wind their torcher and growling that follows behind them.)

Natasha: This is so stupid!

Natasha: Nothing will happen if we look back.

Brent: Natasha! Please stop and keep moving!

Natasha: No! I will prove to you that there is nothing there.

(Everyone is face forward. Natasha is behind them.)

Mia: Please don't do this!

Natasha: I do what I want to do! I will show you all!

Jason: Guy's don't look back…Please keep moving. We are almost there. Just hold on.

Brent: Natasha, baby…please don't do this. We need you.

Natasha: That's why I am doing this…because you'll need me to show you the truth.

Brent: Natasha!! No!!!

(Natasha turns around, while everyone else is still looking forward.)

Natasha: See. I told you nothing will happen if I look back.

(Suddenly Natasha sees these ghostly creatures. She screams

as these ghostly figures snatches her soul from her body. It is like these creatures are feeding on her soul.)

(Brent screams in pain and so do the kids.)

Jason: We must keep moving!

(Brent falls to his knees as tears run down his face. Mia grabs the kids and keeps moving forward. Jason pulls Brent back on his feet.)

Jason: We need to move now.

(The ghostly creature is moving closer and closer again.)

Brent: I can't. I'm so tired.

Jason: I understand, but you have these two beautiful kids who need you more than ever.

Brent: You are right!

(Brent and Jason catch up to Mia and the kids. Mia and the kids stop moving.)

Jason: Mia, why have you stopped?

Mia: Look.

(Mia pointes to the Valley.)

Mia: Jason. Love. We made it.

(The only thing Brent could do is hold his kids tightly.)

Brent: Kids we made it.

Kid 1: So, we can look back)

Brent: Literally yes. Metaphorically, no we can never look back on what was. Only look forward to what's to come. Never forget mom. We will honor her by living the best life and do our best to always do right.

(Everyone walks off into the light.)

Old Macdonald

We are lost.

(It is raining hard and dark. Raymond and his wife Melissa are driving singing their favorite song by Dru Hill "Beauty".)

Melissa: Bae, this song also gets me there.

(Raymond smiles.)

Raymond: Get you where?

Melissa: Boy get your mine out the gutter.

(Melissa blushes. Raymond turns down the radio a little.)

Raymond: Is this the right way?

Melissa: I'm not sure. I never came this way, but the GPS says it's a shorter distance this way.

Raymond: It would be great if it was not raining so hard.

Melissa: I know right.

(They drive another two miles. I figure just thirty yards ahead of them runs across the street. Raymond leans forward to see what that was while driving.)

Raymond: What was that? Melissa, did you see that?

Melissa: See what?

Raymond: It was like a man running across the street ahead.

Melissa: I did not see anything. But it could have been.

(They drive another mile. Suddenly, their front tire blew out. And they spun out of control and nearly ran off the road, but Raymond got control and was able to stop the car.)

Raymond: What the hell. These are brand new tires. Melissa are you okay.

(Melissa holds her chest.)

Melissa: Yes, just a little spook. I did not see anything on the road.

Raymond: I'm going to check and see what happened.

Melissa: I am coming out too.

Raymond: No, stay here. It's raining hard. I can handle this.

Melissa: My hero, but I am coming out too. I can watch your

back.

(Raymond and Melissa both laugh.)

Melissa: We are a team remember.

(Raymond smiles.)

Raymond: Right!

(Raymond grabs a flashlight from the glove compartment. Melissa grabs the umbrella. They both exit the car. They look at the driver's front wheel. Raymond sees a weird object sticking out of the tire.)

Raymond: What is this?

Melissa: I don't know. Can you pull it out?

(Raymond gives the flashlight to Melissa so he can pull out the object from the tire. He pulls it out and holds it to the light.)

Melissa: Is that a claw or nail?

Raymond: It looks like it. But, to what animal?

Melissa: Maybe a bear.

Raymond: It could be, but there are no bears around here.

(They hear a noise coming from the woods.)

Raymond: Did you hear that?

Melissa: Yes, let's get back in the car. We can call AAA for help.

Raymond: Yup, let's do that.

(Raymond quickly walks Melissa to the other side of the car. Melissa gets in. Raymond heads back to his side. Melissa pulls her phone out and tries to call AAA.)

Melissa: Bae, come on in. I am not able to get through. My phone doesn't have a signal…Raymond?

(Raymond doesn't answer her.)

Melissa: Raymond, where are you?

(Still no answer. She looks around out of each window. Raymond is nowhere to be found. She gets out of the car in the rain. Melissa does not see Raymond. She calls for him. Unknowingly, a few yards back Raymond is lying on the side of the road and then gets quickly dragged off. Melissa gets back in the car and tries to call him. While she was doing this something burst through the window. She screams and it pulls her out of the car into the woods. You can hear her scream in the world and suddenly the screaming stops.)

Tournament

(The bobcats are at the end of their Archery tournament. Mason, the team captain and best archer on the team is up next. He lines up next to the other three opponents. The bobcats have been trialing behind the whole tournament. Mason needs a perfect three shots just to put his team in second place.)

(Coach Smith walking over to mason.)

Coach Smith: Mason, you got this. Remember you are the best. Seize this moment.

(Mason nods at Coach Smith.)

Teammates: You got this Mason!! Let's go!

Teammates: No, pressure! Show them what you are capable of!

(Mason rotates his head side to side and rotates his shoulders to loosen up. He takes a couple of deep breaths.)

Mason: Okay Mason, we can get this done.

(Announcer calls for the archers to get ready. All four of them line up side by side with about ten feet of space between them. The announcer tells them to get ready. All four opponents get in their stands. Arrows up, arms are position. The announcer gives them the cue to aim and fire. Mason takes a deep breath and as he releases the arrow, his team freezes…everything seem to move in slow motion. Mason felt good when he shot the arrow. He closed his eyes and smiled. When he opens his eyes, he sees the opponent next to him celebrating. Mason arrow was just two centimeters from the bull's eye. He looks over to his team and their heads are down, some of the teammates have their hands behind their head in disbelief. Mason is the best on the team and ninety-five percent of the time he hits the target right in the middle.)

Disappointment

(Coach Smith and his archery team just finished a

tournament. They are not thrilled with their performance during the competition. They came in third place. The team is now boarding the bus to head back home.)

(Coach Smith speaks to the bus driver.)

Bus Driver: How did it go?

(Coach Smith shakes his head.)

Bus Driver: That bad?

Coach Smith: We could have done much better. It's like we forgot all our training.

Bus Driver: Were they nervous?

Coach Smith: Nervous! Have the team been to this level of competition. I tell you what it is…they are not focus.

(Team is boarding the bus. Everyone is quiet.)

(Mason who is the team captain and one of the best archeries on the team. Mason also failed to lead his team to victory.)

Jeff: Mason, what happened to you out there?

(Mason looks up at Jeff and turns back around.)

Jeff: Oh, so you have nothing to say ah?

Zoe: Leave him alone Jeff.

Jeff: Why? He's been riding us and acting like he is above us this whole time…Just to shit on himself at the most important moment.

(Mason Jumps up and shoving Jeff…Jeff pushes him back. Now the whole team is riled up.)

Mason: Kept it up and I am going to beat the shit out of you.

(Coach Smith and the assistant coach Neal break through to stop everything.)

Coach Smith: What the hell is going on!

Mason: Nothing!

Jeff: Nothing!

Coach Smith: Nothing! No something is going on.

Jeff: Just asking our fearless leader what happened out there.

Coach Smith: What happen? I'll tell you what happen…All of you performed terrible out there.

Coach Smith: You all got too comfortable out there…We barely made it to third place. I don't know what it will take for you all to work together as a team and show support for each other.

(The team looks at each other during the Coach smith speech.)

(Khole another teammate looks back at some of her teammates from the front of the bus.)

Coach Smith: We have a three-hour ride back home. Why don't you all take the time to build each other up? Figure out how to improve…Some of you this is it. We have one more tournament next week. We can win this.

(Jaron another teammate is setting across from Mason. Jaron turns Mason direction and shakes his head.)

(Mason stares off into the window.)

(Jaron whispered to his teammate.)

Jaron: It is too many selfish people on this team.

(Teammate said right to Jaron.)

(Bus pulls off.)

New Path

(Three-hour ride back home. The team was on the road for an hour. Some teammates are sleeping. Others, are having side conversation.)

(Zoe moves closer to Mason. Mason has headphones in his ear. Zoe taps him.)

Zoe: Hey.

(Mason takes headphones out his ear.)

Mason: Hey, what's up.

Zoe: You good?

Mason: Yeah.

Zoe: So, what happened?

Mason: What do you mean?

Zoe: You always hit your targets. I've never really seen you off by much. It's like you were somewhere else.

Mason: Look, I'm good. It was just one of those days.

Mason: I'll be ready for finals.

Zoe: Good. The team needs you to tap in. Plus, Khole, Jeff and I really need to do great as a team. This can help us all with a scholarship.

Mason: Well, very one needs to step up then. Instead of depending on one person.

(Mason said this in a sarcastic way.)

Zoe: Wow, that's how you feel Mason?
Mason: Yeah, that's how I feel.
Zoe: You know, you can be a real a-hole at times.
Mason: Do this a-hole a favorite and go back to your seat.
(Zoe gets up with an irritating look.)
Zoe: Screw you Mason.
(Zoe heads back to her seat.)
(Bus driver calls Coach Smith. Coach gets up and sees that the driver wanted.)
Coach Smith: How is it going?
Bus Driver: Everything is good…I just seen on my GPS that there is another route that can get you guys' home 30 minutes earlier.
Coach Smith: Oh really?
Bus Driver: Yes sir. So, what do you think?
Coach Smith: Yeah, let's do it. I need to get them home as quickly as possible. Before they kill themselves.
(Bus Driver and Coach Smith laugh.)
Bus Driver: Detour it is.

Detour

(Bus driver takes eerie path. There are no other cars on this road. Something strange is in the air. Students look puzzled as to what direction the bus driver is going.)
Jeff: Hey! Coach Smith.
Coach Smith: Yes, Jeff.
Jeff: Um…This is not the route we took coming.
Coach Smith: I know…This is a faster route. We will be home in half an hour quicker.
Jeff: Oh word!
Jeff: It just seems a little weird.
Max: What's some matter bro…You scared?
Jeff: Shut-up and go back to sleep.
(Jeff gives Max the finger.)
Coach Neal: Is this a good idea to take this route?
Coach Smith: Yes, I mean what's the worst that can happen?
Coach Smith: This is the quickest way home.
(They have been driving on this path for 30 minutes. There is something strange about this direction.)

(Mason stares out the window. He has this feeling as if they are being watched by something or someone.)

Max: Mason, why are you staring so hard through the window?

Mason: I don't know man…I have this weird feeling of being watch.

Jaron: Maybe it's the wrong turn (Jaron Laughs).

Khole: Shut up Jaron.

Jaron: What?

Jaron: He never seen the wrong turn movies?

Khole: I don't do scary movies, it's for lames.

Jaron: Yo momma a lame.

Khole: Punk! Yo momma a lame

(Next thing happen one of the front tires is blown out. The bus driver loses control and runs off road into a tree. The team got shaken by the crash.)

Bus Driver: Everyone hang on!

(Coach Smith checks on everyone.)

Coach Smith: Is everyone good!

(Team sounds off.)

Coach Smith: What the hell happened?

Bus Driver: I don't know. We must have run over something sharp.

Coach Smith: Can we fix it?

Bus Driver: Yes, if we have a spare tire.

Coach Neal: We can call someone.

Coach Smith: Yes. Let's call for help.

(They all check their cell phones.)

Coach Neal: I'm not getting a signal.

Bus Driver: Yeah, I not getting a signal either.

Coach Smith: This is strange. I don't have a signal either.

(They look out the front window.)

Jeff: Hey, Coach Smith what's going on?

Coach Smith: Hey, everything will be okay.

Zoe: Coach is anyone coming for help.

Coach Smith: Zoe we are taking care of it. Just set tight. Help is coming.

(Coach Neal whispered to Coach Smith.)

Coach Neal: Coach, we need to find help quickly. None of

the cell phones are working.

Coach Smith: We are going to have to walk and find help. We are still close to the road. We can just follow it until we get to the next town or find a house who can help.

Bus Driver: I can go and find help.

Coach Smith: I can go with you. Neal stays with the kids. We'll come back with help.

Coach Smith: Hey guys, we are about to go get help. Coach Neal will be here with you all. No one gets off this bus.

Coach Smith: Mason, come here really quick.

Mason: Yes coach.

Coach Smith: Hey, I need you to help lead your team. Help Coach Neal.

Mason: Coach, they are not going to listen to me.

Coach Smith: Mason, well you must make this listen to you. Find a way to lead them. Great leaders always find away. Mason, it is team to change your mind set.

(Mason looks on at his teammates as this are trying to figure out what is going on.)

(Coach and the Bus driver gets off the bus. They go and check out the blown tire. They are both shocked at what they find.)

Bus Driver: What is that in the tire.

Coach Smith: It looks like a claw or something like that.

Bus Driver: From what a bear?

Coach Smith: I don't believe there are bears around here.

(The team looks out the window to see what they are looking at.)

Jeff: Why do they have a consider look on their face?

Coach Neal: I don't know but let's make sure we all stay inside.

(They watch the bus driver and Coach Smith walk off for help.)

Someone Please Help

(Coach Smith and Bus Driver is walking on the side of the road.)

Coach Smith: Did you see any animals laying on the road?

Bus Driver: I did not see anything, a clear road. It's like

something shot at the tires.

Coach Smith: What would shoot out a fingernail that looks like it came from a dinosaur?

Bus Driver: Good question.

(They stable across a house. They move closer to see if anyone is home.)

Bus Driver: Look, there is a house.

Coach Smith: Maybe someone can help.

(They're now at the front porch and knock.)

Coach Smith: Hello! Hello!

Coach Smith: I don't think anyone is home or lives here.

Bus Driver: Wait! I think I saw someone.

Coach Smith: What?

Bus Driver: Man! I saw someone in there.

(Coach knocks again.)

Coach Smith: Hello! Hey, we need some help. We just need to use your phone please.

(No one answered.)

(They hear a noise like someone stepping on sticks. They both turn around.)

Bus Driver: Did you hear that?

Coach Smith: Yes, I did.

(They stare out into the woods waiting for someone of something to come out. Next, they hear the door open slowly behind them. They look at each other…And slash across the Bus Driver face. He falls down screaming! Coach Smith falls off the porch. It grabs Bus driver and pulls him in. Coach Smith runs back up the porch and grabs his hands and ends up in a tug of war.)

(Bus Driver screams as he feels his body ripping in half.)

(Coach Smith is losing his grip with Bus driver.)

Bus Driver: Help!!! Help!!!

(He, his screams.)

(It pulls even harder…Coach Smith is pulled to the door. It slashes Coach arm. He lets go and falls back. It snatches the Bus Driver in quickly and the door close…He hears screams, and the screams begins to fade.)

(Door opens back up. Coach Smith immediately jumps up and takes off running. As he is running, he can hear it running after him. While running a fingernail was shot at him but missed and hit the tree.)

(He runs and runs. He finally sees the bus front the back. He is about sixty yards away from the bus. Right when he tries to run towards the bus, it tackles him and drags him off.)

(The whole time the team is oblivious to what is going on.)

Where are They

(It's been an hour now and everyone is starting restless.)

Zoe: Where are they? It's been over an hour.

Mason: Coach Neal, you thinking something happened to them?

Coach Neal: I'm sure they are okay. As a matter of fact I bet they are on their way back.

Max: Mason, Coach Smith and the bus driver were looking at something that got the spook.

(Mason gets up and heads to the door.)

Coach Neal: Mason! Wait! Where are you going?

(Mason looks back and turns back towards the door.)

Jeff: What the hell with this…I'm coming too.

(Everyone gets off the bus to see what Coach Smith and the bus driver were looking at.)

Coach Neal: Hey! Wait! We should all stay on the bus.

(Mason and his team go and look at the tire. Mason pulls the claw out of the tire.)

Khole: Is that a claw?

Jaron: What did we hit?

(Jaron stands in the middle of the road.)

Coach Neal: Okay guys! Let's get back on the bus.

(Coash Neal is trying to get everyone back on the bus. A loud roar echoed to the bus. Everyone quiet and look around.)

Zoe: What is that?

Coach Neal: Okay Okay…Let go back now everyone…Now!

(Everyone runs back on the bus. Coach Neal quickly closes the door once everyone is on.)

Mason: Coach, what was that?

Coach Neal: I don't know…How would I know?

(Everyone is looking out the windows. They see nothing.)

Zoe: Look look!

Mason: What?
Zoe: Someone was standing there by the trees.
Mason: I don't see anyone.
Zoe: I am telling you someone was there.
(Everyone is still trying to figure out what that noise was, and Zoe is very convinced that something is watching them.)
Jeff: Aye let's check our cell phones.
(Everyone checks their cellphones.)
Khole: Nothing.
Mason: Nothing.
Jaron: Nothing.
(Something brushes against the bus.)
Khole: What was that.
Coach Neal: Shhh!
(Everyone is quiet. Silence so thick you can cut it.)
(Again, something brushes against the bus.)
(While everyone is looking out each window. Zoe slowly turns and sees things looking at her. She screams! Everyone turns around scared.)
Mason: What! What do you see?
Zoe: It was there! Some sort of man creature.
Jaron: What! That doesn't make since…A creature man?
Coach Neal: Okay everyone calm down.
Jeff: Calm down! Something is out their coach.
Jaron: Maybe someone should go out there and check.
(Everyone looks at Jaron crazy.)
Mason: We are in the middle of nowhere. If something is out there, I feel the best thing to do is wait.
Jeff: Wait for what? It has been two hours, and I have not seen any other cars driving down this road.
Coach Neal: Mason is right. We stay put. Plus, it is almost dark.
Mason: And where will we go? We don't even know where we are at.
(Bus shakes! Everyone screams! It rams against the bus multiple times. It breaks windows, shakes the bus.)
Mason: Everyone grab your bows!

Fight or Die.

(Everyone grabs their bows and aims at the windows. It's quiet again.)

Mason: Where is it?

Jaron: It's gone! Maybe it was just a deer.

Jeff: Shut up! What deer you know do something like this?

Mason: Shhh! Something is…

(Bus shakes! It burst through a window and grabbed one of the teammates and pulled her out. Everyone fired their bows aim at where the creature was. They tried to help.)

(Everyone is screaming.)

Jeff: What the hell was that?

Mason: Keep firing!

(Behind them another comes and bursts through another window grabs another teammate pulls him out. More screams!)

Mason: Coach, what should we do?

Coach Neal: Keep firing!!

Mason: It's more than one!

(Another one busts through the back door.)

Coach Neal: Everyone off the bus! Now!

(Everyone runs off the bus and flees to the woods.)

(They ran and ran and run, until they came across the house. An old farm house.)

Mason: Look, there is a house.

Jeff: Is this a farm?

(Roar reaches them from the woods.)

Coach Neal: Someone should be home to help.

Mason: I don't know coach…I don't think we should go in.

Coach Neal: It can't be worse than what's out here.

(They rush to the front door. They knock and scream for help.)

Nowhere is Safe

(Door opens. They look suspicious.)

Khole: Should we go in?

Mason: We don't have a choice.

(They walk in slowly. Looking around. Hello…Hello, everyone said.)

Zoe: This place looks abandoned.

Jaron: Look at these creepy pictures.

Coach Neal: Where are the creatures at?
Zoe: I don't understand…It's like they are some kind of reptile looking wolf monster.
Jaron: Wow, your imagination is wild.
Mason: Well, what do you think it is then geniuses?
Coach Neal: Hey, let's chill on that and find a phone that works.
Mason: Maybe we should split up.
Coach Neal: Yes, that's a good idea.
Zoe: I can go with you Mason.
Coach Neal: Okay Jeff you and Khole…and Jaron you with me.
Jaron: Oh great…How I get stuck with you.
Coach Neal: Shut up and let's go.
(They break off into three groups. Searching through the house for a phone.)
(Coach Neal and Jaron head to the basement. Mason and Zoe head upstairs. Khole and Jeff check the kitchen and rooms on the main floor.)
Zoe: Mason, who do you think used to live here?
Mason: Who or what…I not sure.
Zoe: What do you mean?
Mason: Look at these pictures. Look at their eyes. They are black.
Zoe: Mason, I don't think we should be in this house.
Mason: You are right…Let's go!
(As they return around, there it is. Sharp long nails. Teeth large and sharp like knives. Scales like a lizard with fur. Standing at the door, blocking the way.)
(Mason quickly aims the bow and takes the shot. He hits the creature on the shoulder. It lets out a loud roar scream.)
(Everyone else in the house hears it.)
Jaron: What the hell was that?
Coach Smith: It's in here.
(Coach Smith and Jaron try to run back up to see what's going on, but there is another creature blocking them from coming up.)
(They shoot an arrow and miss. It runs and slashes at Jaron, cutting him across the face. Coach hits it with nearby chair. It

turns around and knocks the coach down. Jaron shoots another arrow, this time hitting it in the lower back.)

(It roars loud! Turns around hold its hand up and shoot a nail from its finger right into the neck of Jaron.)

(Coach gets up and Jumps on the back of it stabbing multiple times in the neck and side. It throws the coach off its back, grabs him and bits him on the shoulder. Coach screams.)

(Jeff and Khole run down and shoot another arrow hitting it right in the head. It gets up and tries to run over, and Khole puts another arrow in its head.)

(Finally, it falls and dies. They rush over to Coach Neal. They help him up.)

Coach Neal: I'm okay, check on Jaron.

(They rush over to Jaron.)

Jeff: Coach, His…his gone.

(Back upstairs Mason and Zoe are fighting for their lives.)

(Mason shoots an arrow. He hits the creature on the shoulder. It knocks it out and shoots a claw at Mason…missing him, but hits Zoe in the leg.)

(It runs over and picks Mason up and slams him down. Zoe tries to jump up and shoots another arrow, hitting it on the side.)

(It gets up and slashes Mason on the chest, next it runs over, and Jeff comes in and shoots an arrow in the neck of the creature. It falls.)

(Mason runs over to Zoe.)

Mason: Zoe!

Zoe: I'm okay…It just buns a little.

(Mason pulls the claw out. Zoe screams a little. He tied her wound up.

Coach and Khole made it up stairs.)

Jeff: What the hell is that!

Coach Neal: I'm not sure…They look like some kind of wolf/lizard.

Khole: I found this old piece of mail. The name on it is the Macdonald family.

Jeff: You must be kidding me!

Jeff: That really says the Macdonald family.

Khole: Yes. There is a letter in said too.

Mason: Let me see that.
Mason: It says that this land is now owned by the bank. They lost their farm.
Jeff: So, this is literally Old Macdonald farm?
Jeff: I hate nursery rhythms!
Coach Neal: We need to get out of here. We don't know how many more of these things are out there.
Mason: You don't think these things are the family?
Zoe: What are you saying? They turn into these creatures. How is that possible?

Time to Escape

(Everyone heads back downstairs to regroup.)
(As they make it to the kitchen, Zoe grabs her leg.)
Mason: Zoe! Are you okay?
Zoe: No…My leg is burning.
(Coach Neal sits down and grabs his neck and shoulder.)
Jeff: Coach, are you okay too?
Coach Neal: Yeah, I'm just hot a little.
Khole: Coach, let me see your bites.
(Khole checks Coach Neals bites and she is disturbing by what she sees.)
Coach Neal: What is it.
(Mason comes over and looks. His eyes get big. Mason looks at Khole.)
Coach Neal: What is it.
(They hear a loud boom from down the hall.)
Mason: One of them is inside!
Mason: Zoe can you walk?
Zoe: Yes, I should be fine.
(Coach gets up.)
Coach Neal: We can go out the back.
Mason: Let's go!
(Everyone rushes out the back. They run and see the barn house. The creature is behind them moving fast. They run into the barn house to hind.)
(Jeff keeps running looking for a place to hide in the barn. He trips over something. Jeff sets up and sees lying there Coach Smith half eaten.)

(Jeff jumps up scared with blood from the body on him. He runs into Mason.)

Mason: Jeff, what happened? Where did this blood come from?

Jeff: I…I found Coach Smith.

Mason: Where?

Jeff: Over there.

(Mason walks over and sees Coach Smith half eaten body. Zoe limps over to Mason. She sees it too and almost screams, until Mason covers her mouth.)

Mason: Shhh! They will hear you.

(Khole whisper help to everyone. Mason rushed over to Khole. Mason sees Khole kneeling on the ground holding her leg.)

Mason: Khole! What's wrong.

(Khole does not answer.)

Mason: Khole.

(Mason whisper. He walks closer to her.)

Mason: Khole?

(Mason reaches out to Khole. As soon as he touches her, she turns around quickly…What he saw, nearly turned him white.)

(Khole eyes are now black. Black veins appeared across her face to her neck. Teeth sharp like knives. Mason jumps back. Khole with a raspy deep voice.)

Khole: What is happening to me!

(Coach Neal screamed out. Jeff runs over to him. The same thing that is happening to Khole is happening to Neal.)

Jeff: Mason! What is going on?

Zoe: They are changed into those things. If they shoot you with their nails or bite you, and you survive…you will turn into these creatures.

(Coach Neal jumps up. Saliva mixed with blood dropping down from his month.)

Jeff: Coach…

(Coach runs at Jeff and tackles him. Jeff calls for help as he is trying to fight off Coach Neal.)

(Mason runs over and knocks coach off him. Coach jumps back up and runs at them both. Jeff picks up a rode and tries to kill him. Coach grabs the rode and slashes his arm knocking him down.)

Mason: Get back!

Zoe: Mason!

(Coach holds his hand out and shoots a nail at them but miss. They continue to fight with him. Khole runs over to help them, even though she is changing too.)

Khole: Go! Run now…I'll hold him off.

Mason: No, come this us.

Khole: Look at me…I'm not going anywhere.

Mason: No, I am staying.

Khole: Go! Now!

(Coach and Khole began to fight. Slashing at each other.)

Jeff: Let's go!

(Zoe pulls on Mason. The other creatures are from hearing all the noise.)

Mason: Khole!

Khole: It's okay Mason…Go now!

Zoe: Mason, we must leave now.

(They run out as the creatures break in the back and side. Khole and coach continue to fight. Khole slashes the coaches' neck and rips his head off.)

(The creatures run at Khole, and she tries to fight them off. As Mason, Jeff and Zoe run out back to the woods they hear a loud roar scream that comes from Khole. Mason stops for a second and looks back.)

(One of the creatures chases after them. Mason shoots an arrow hitting it right in the head. They run and run. Another creature jumps out…Zoe shoots it in the chest. It keeps coming.)

Mason: The head! They fall quicker.

(Jeff takes another shot and hits it right in the head.)

Mason: Come on! We are almost back to the road.

Are we in the clear?

(Running for their lives. Nails from the creature claws fly at them. They run and run…finally made it to the road. Mason turns around and shoots two arrows hitting two of the creatures.)

Zoe: It's amazing.
Mason: What?
Zoe: You have been on point with hitting your targets now.
(They both laugh.)
Jeff: Hey, guys.
(They run to Jeff.)
Jeff: I feel weird.
(Jeff falls to his knees.)
Zoe: Jeff what is it? You look fine.
(Mason walking behind Jeff. Looks at his back and sees three nails in his back.)
Mason: Zoe, look at this.
(Zoe looks at Jeff's back and covers her mouth.)
Jeff: What? What is it?
(Mason and Zoe look sad.)
Jeff: That bad uh?
(Jeff looks down at the ground and smiles.)
Jeff: Well, you know what you need to do right?
Mason: No! We can take you to a hospital.
Zoe: Right. We can stay on this road and follow it back to the tournament.
Jeff: Come on! You both know good and well that I will not make it. Plus, we were driving for over and hour on this road…It will take hours…Hours that neither of us have.

Zoe: Well, it's better than what you are proposing. A car will come as we walk back.
Jeff: Zoe, look at me. I am burning up inside. I don't want to become one of those things.
Zoe: Mason! Talk some sense into him.
Jeff: This is my choice.
Mason: Zoe, he is right.
Zoe: What the hell are you saying?
Zoe: Have lost your mind?
Mason: Zoe, look at him. In ten or fifteen minutes he will turn. Then what?
Jeff: Zoe, please walk off.
(Zoe does not move.)
Jeff: Zoe, now! Walk off!

(Zoe runs over and kisses Jeff on the lips. Jeff smiles.)

Jeff: Oh, what's that for?

Zoe: I should have done this a long time ago.

(Zoe runs off crying.)

Jeff: Mason, let's get this over with.

Mason: I sorry.

Jeff: Sorry for what? You do not cause this.

(Jeff eyes are black, blood coming from his mouth due to knew teeth coming in.)

(Mason pulls back on the bow string.)

Jeff: Don't miss.

(Jeff's smiles.)

(A tear runs down Mason's face. He aims and fires right into Jeff's head.)

(Mason catches up to Zoe.)

Zoe: It's done?

Mason: It is.

Zoe: What do we tell the cops?

Mason: I don't know. No one will believe us.

Zoe: But we have to say something.

Mason: We will…let's get back to the other road and get a ride.

Zoe: I will never go hiking or do anything in the woods again.

Mason: I with you on that…I'm staying in the city forever.

(They both laugh.)

(Behind them another creature runs across the road. They don't know they are being followed.)

Abaddon

Not A Believer

(It is 9:30pm on a Thursday night. Lori and Zack are paramedics on break waiting to be called for medical assistance. They are waiting in the parking lot of a coney island restaurant. Zack is leaving out of coney island with food for Lori and himself. Zack gets into the ambulance.)

Lori: It's about time.

Zack: Man listen, I was about to jump over the counter and make the food myself.

Lori: You weren't going to do anything.

(As she rolls her eyes and laughs.)

Zack: The heck I was! They know I don't play.

Lori: Boy please! You are not tough, and they know it. You stood there looking silly and helpless, while they played around making our food.

Zack: Oh yeah? Well, I tell you what. Next time you go in there and let's see what happens.

(Zack takes a bite into his hamburger.)

Lori: I will. Watch them take only ten minutes while I'm standing there.

Zack: Dawg! Talking to you made me forget to say my blessing.

(Zack puts down his burger, close his eye's and begins to say his blessing.)

Zack: Father in the name of Jesus, thank you for this meal I am about receive…

(Lori frowns at Zack during his blessing over his food.)

Lori: You can't be serious.

(Zack finished his prayer.)

Zack: Let it nourish my mind, body, and soul.

(Zack opens his eyes. Lori is staring directly in his face.)

Zack: What?!

Lori: What? What was that?
Zack: Um…me thanking God before I eat. Why? Is there a problem?
(Zack takes a sip of his pop while looking at Lori.)
Lori: Well first, don't look at me like that while sipping any drink. Secondly, you praying over greasy unhealthy food is wild.
Zack: What do you mean?
(Zack looks at his burger.)
Zack: It has vegetables, pickles, lettuce and tomatoes. Protein, the beef patty, and starch bread buns. All healthy stuff in one.
(Zack smiles at the burger and takes another bite.)
(Lori takes a sip of her pop and looks at Zack.)
Lori: You think you are so clever uh?
Zack: Yup!
Lori: And third, you praying is not going to stop you from getting fat and sick.
(Zack smacks his lips and leans back in his seat.)
Zack: I see what this is.
Lori: You see what?
Zack: Yup. Makes perfect sense.
Lori: What?
Zack: You don't believe in God. Like who sits there and ridicules someone for saying their prayers.
(Lori hunches her shoulders and points to herself.)
Lori: Stop doing weird stuff and you won't be ridicule…and who goes around saying ridicule away.
(Zack looks forward out the front window and shakes his head.)
Zack: Tell me you are an atheist, without telling me you are an atheist.
(Lori eats a fry and looks at Zack with a smile.)
Lori: Aye, don't get mad at me because you believe in fairy tales.
Zack: It's not fair tales' loser!
Lori: Yo mama a loser!
Zack: Yo mama a loser!
(Lori turns in her seat to face Zack.)
Lori: Please explain to me how God is real?

Zack: How is God real you ask?
Lori: Well, speak!
Zack: Girl you get one more time here.
(Lori rolls her eyes.)
Zack: Alright. God is real like the air we breathe. Like gravity that holds us down. You cannot see air or gravity, but you know it's there doing its job keeping us alive and keeping us grounded.
Lori: See. You just messed up.
Zack: How?
Zack: Can you see both?
Lori: No. But you can feel air against your face. Gravity is force that pulls or holds you down physically.
Zack: And God is all of that.
Lori: You can feel air, even though you can not see it…Where is God and why can't you see or feel him.
Zack: You can feel and see God if you open that dark heart of yours.
(Lori looks up with her hands up.)
Lori: God! Oh God…Are you there?
Zack: See the problem is you think you're funny.
Lori: Oh God! If you are there make my fries float.
(Lori laughs.)
Zack: Keep playing with him.
(Lori leans over to Zack.)
Lori: Look, feel this.
(Lori blows her breath in Zack's face. Zack leans back away from Lori and covers his nose.)
Zack: Move! Your breath stinks!
(Lori raises her hand up in a slapping gesture way.)
Lori: Shut up, before I slap you.
Zack: You may not believe in God, but the devil definitely lives in your mouth.
(Lori swings at Zack in a playful way.)
Lori: Keep playing with me boy.

The Call
(Dispatch calls in for an elderly injured woman from a fall in her house.)

Dispatch: Hey guy's, we receive a call about an elderly woman injured in a fall at her home. She's fallen and she can't get up.

(Zack laughs at the falling and she can't get up.)

Lori: Hush…

Dispatch: Can you go and give medical attention.

Lori: Sure. We are heading there now. What's the address?

Dispatch: 7739 Grands St.

Lori: Copy that.

Dispatch: Thank you…We'll be waiting for you.

(Lori looked confused from the last statement dispatch said.)

Lori: What?

(She pauses for a second.)

Lori: Zack did you hear that?

(Zack adjusted his seat belt.)

Zack: Hear what?

Lori: The last thing dispatch said.

(Zack looks at Lori weird.)

Zack: Um…yes. She said, thank you and be safe.

(Lori looks at Zack and then looks at the radio and just shook her head.)

Zack: You alright?

Lori: Yeah, I'm good.

(They pull out from the parking lot and proceed to head there. As they are driving, Lori is still thinking about that statement.)

Lori: I wonder who called 911 for the lady.

Zack: What do you mean?

Lori: Like, who called? Was it a grandchild, husband, or roommate…or someone.

Zack: Does it matter who called?

Lori: Normally dispatch would say who called, so we know to talk to them.

Zack: Yeah, that's true. I guess we'll find out when we get there.

(They pulled up to the house. It is a big creepy looking house. Lori and Zack looked at each other and gave each other a nod. They get out of the ambulance, grab their equipment needed.)

Zack: Alright, showtime.

(Both Lori and Zack head to the front door. Lori hesitates to knock.)

Lori: Why is it dark inside.

Zack: Um…I don't know.

(Lori knocks on the door.)

Lori: Hello.

(Lori knocks again.)

Lori: Hello…We are the paramedics. We were called for an elderly lady who maybe injured.

(No one answers. Lori looks back at Zack. Zack shrugged his shoulders. Lori turns around and knocks again. This time when she knocks again, the door slightly opens. Lori looks puzzled. She hesitates before walking in. Lori slowly pushes the door open a little more.)

Lori: Hello…Ma'am. Is anyone here?

(Lori and Zack turn on their flashlights and walk in. They began to look around for anyone who may be injured and call out to see if anyone would respond.)

Zack and Lori: Hello…

Zack: We are EMT, here to help. Call out if you can.

Lori: Zack you look over there and I'll go this way and look.

Zack: Hell no! I'm not splitting up.

Lori: What a punk! Ain't nothing going to happen to you.

Zack: Girl, I seen this movie! No, we are not splitting up. We stick together. Plus, if anyone or thing jumps out at me, I'll have you to push in the way so I can escape.

(Lori flashes her light in Zack's face. Zack covers his eyes to block the light.)

Zack: Aye! What the hell!

Lori: For someone who believes in God, you sure do say hell a lot.

Zack: Well, hell is in the bible and God says it.

Lori: Um… I don't think it works like that.

(During their back and forth, in the living room there is a small figure standing in the dark with a smile. All you can see is yellowish brown teeth. Lori and Zack are both unaware that something is standing right there watching them.)

Zack: And what do you know. God is nothing more than a

fairy tale.

(As they are talking, they both hear moaning coming from the kitchen.)

Lori: You hear that?

Zack: Yes, it's coming from the kitchen.

Lori: Ma'am, keep calling out.

(Lori and Zack rush over to the kitchen and see the elderly woman lying on the floor. Lori gets down to check her pulse.)

Lori: She's breathing, but barely breathing.

Zack: Damn! I forgot the intubation. I'm going to run and get it.

Lori: Okay, I'll watch her. Ms. You are in good hands.

(Zack runs out of the house to retrieve the intubation. Lori looks at her watch to see the time. It is 11:58)

We Finally Meet

(Lori remembers she has intubation in her bag. She takes it out of her bag and puts it over the lady's face to help with air flow. Lori jumps up and rushes to the door to let Zack know she has the intubation. She tries to open the door, but it will not budge.)

Lori: What the hell! Why is this door locked?

(Lori keeps trying to open the door. Lori yells for Zack!)

Lori: Zack! Zack! The door won't open. Zack!

(Zack is still searching for the intubation. He does not hear her calls. Lori tries a few more times getting the door open before she decides to try the side door.)

Lori: Okay, let me try the side door.

(As soon as she turns around, the elderly lady is standing right behind her. Lori jumps back against the door. She's shocked at what she sees. The elderly lady is standing there smiling, holding a tray with coffee and crackers. Lori steps to the side slowly. The elderly lady stood there staring at the door, still smiling, and holding the tray. Her teeth are a dark tan color.)

Lori: Ma'am are you okay?

(Lori proceeds to wave her hand in front of her eyes.)

Lori: Hello.

(Lady finally snaps out of it. At that moment of snapping out

of her gaze, Lori jumps back.)
Elderly Lady: Oh, pardon me sweetheart.
(She giggles.)
Elderly Lady: Sometimes I tend to stare off into the a bliss…Coffee and crackers?
(Lori does not know what to say. When she does speak, she begins to stutter.)
Lori: Mm Ms. Are you okay?
Elderly Lady: What do you mean dear?
Lori: You were laid out on the floor, barely breathing.
Elderly Lady: Well…I'm good now.
(Lori looks out the door window for Zack.)
Elderly Lady: Oh, don't worry about Zack. We won't be needing him.
(Lori turns around with a scared look on her face.)
Lori: What?
Elderly Lady: We will not be needing him.
(She walks over to the dining room table.)
Elderly Lady: Come, sit with me. We've been waiting for you.
Lori: Who is we? What are you talking about?
(Lori looks back out of the door window. Zack has no clue what is going on as he keeps looking for the intubation. Lori turns back around.)
Lori: Ma'am, I really believe you need some help. Unlock this door and we can get you the proper help.
Elderly Lady: Come, sit with me, and have a chat. After our conversation, I'll unlock the door.
(The elderly lady extended her hand towards the chair for Lori to sit.)

Who Are We

(Lori takes a step forward and then hesitates for a second. Then walk over slowly. The elderly lady still has this creepy and pale face. She stares at Lori as if she could see into her soul. Lori walks over and pulls the seat out and slowly sits down. Lori puts both her hands on the table. Lori calmly speaks.)
Lori: Ma'am, what's going on?
(Elderly lady says nothing. She just stares at Lori with a big

smile. Head slightly tilted down. She then snapped out of it, at the same time startled Lori.)

Elderly Lady: Oh no…Looks like we block out again.

(She laughs.)

Lori: Ma'am, who is we? Is someone else here with you?

Elderly Lady: Oh silly, we are all here. Right in front of you, please call me Abaddon.

(She leans in towards Lori, head slightly tilted. Lori leans back in her seat.)

Lori: Abaddon?

Abaddon: Yes, Abaddon is the name. I am a demon and I have been stuck in this old rotten flesh for 50 years. Until she dies, I'm stuck here.

(Lori bust out laughing.)

Lori: A demon? Really? Who is this person you are stuck in?

Abaddon: Yes. Her name is Peggy.

Lori: Abaddon or Peggy you are not in your right state of mind. I believe you may be dealing with some form of Alzheimer's.

Abaddon: That's right. You are an atheist. You believe in nothing…at least for now.

(Lori shrugs her shoulders.)

Abaddon: Invite me in and allow me to use you.

Lori: You want me to believe you are a demon. Well, try to possess me. If you can, then you can use me for whatever you want.

(Abaddon stares at Lori with a serious look. As if it was really trying to possess Lori. A few seconds go by, and nothing happen. Lori looks around and shakes her head.)

Lori: Yup, I felt nothing. Some demon you are.

(Lori laughs. Abaddon looks frustrated.)

Abaddon: Don't gloat.

(Lori stands up and the seat is pushed back.)

Lori: Listen lady or Abaddon. I don't know what game you are trying to play, but you got the wrong person.

(Lori starts walking out of the dining room and tries to call for Zack on the walkie-talkie. Nothing comes through but static.)

Lori: Zack! Zack, can you hear me? Zack come in!

(Static.)

(A voice comes in but it's not Zack's voice nor is it Abaddon voice. The voice is another woman crying for help.)

Woman voice: Hello! Please help me! Please!

(Lori looks at her walkie-talkie confused at to what she is hearing. Lori slightly looks back towards Abaddon and then looks back at the walkie-talkie.)

Lori: Who is this?

Woman voice: Please help me! They are ripping me apart.

Lori: What? Where are you?

(Woman screams out.)

Woman voice: I'm here! I'm here!

(The woman goes quiet. The only thing Lori hears now is static again. Next, another voice comes through and this time it's a creepy voice…the voice of Abaddon.)

Abaddon: Come back and sit down.

(Lori drops the walkie-talkie. Steps back, then runs to the door. Banging and calling for Zack, but he cannot hear her. She runs pass Abaddon thru the kitchen to the side door. Abaddon sits there with a smile. Lori bangs and tries to push the side door open multiple times. She screams in hoping Zack will hear her. She stops and turns around. Abaddon is standing there. Lori falls back against the door with a frightening look on her face.)

Lori: What the hell!

Abaddon: Shall we try the back door next?

(Abaddon smiles knowing that the back door will not open either.)

Lori: What do you want?

Abaddon: As of right now, just want to talk. I'll let you know soon what we want.

(Abaddon turns around and walks back to the dining room table. Lori stood by the door and watched Abaddon walk back to the dining room table. Lori hears her sitting down and scooting her chair. She slowly walks over to the table. Lori stands there for a second staring at Abaddon and then sits down.)

Lori: Okay, so now what?

Abaddon: Why are you a quitter?

Lori: Excuse me?
Lori: Quit what?
(Lori is confused. Abaddon slightly looks up and then looks back at Lori.)
Abaddon: Um…Everything.
(Lori grows frustrated.)
Lori: Look here Abaddon. I don't know what you think this is or who you think I am…But you are too old for pranks.
(Abaddon laughs.)
Abaddon: No pranks dear. We know everything about you.
Lori: Enough!
(Lori pulls out her cell phone.)
Lori: I'm calling the cops.
Abaddon: Go right ahead.
(Lori calls the cops.)
911: 911 what's your emergency?
Lori: Please send someone to 7739 Brand St. I am being held hostage against my will.
911: Okay Lori, we will send someone over.
(Lori looks at her phone with a shock look and pauses.)
Lori: I never told you, my name.
(Abaddon is just sitting there staring with a smile.)
911: Just have a conversation with us.
Lori: What?
(911 voice repeats talk to us repeatedly in a raspy voice.)
911: Talk to us. Talk to us. Talk to us!
(Lori drops the phone and looks at Abaddon.)
Abaddon: Shall we proceed?
Lori: What do you want from me?
Abaddon: You like to write?
Lori: Yes, sometimes.
Abaddon: You are an excellent writer. You had a full ride to Howard University, right?
(Lori looks puzzled.)
Lori: Yes, but how do you know this. Who are you really?
Abaddon: I told you who I am, and we know everything.
Lori: Stop with the damn games!
(Abaddon claps her hands softly and fast.)
Abaddon: I like games. I have a game. Let's see what else we

know about you.
(Lori jumps up and points at Abaddon.)
Lori: Listen! You little creep. You don't know anything about me.
(The lights in the kitchen began to flicker. It catches Lori attention. Lori has a curious and fearful look. She looks back at Abaddon.)
Abaddon: Lori, born April 10th in 1987 in Detroit, Michigan. Parents are Mary and John Ray. At 10 years old, your mother died. Father did the best he could to raise you, but it wasn't enough for you. Honor role student your whole life. You love to write and received a full ride scholarship to Howard University. Dropped out your second year to take care of your father. Never married. Single only a month now. You push David away because you don't see a future with him.
(Lori can't believe what she is hearing. How does a person she has never met know so much about her. Who is she? So many thoughts are going through her head.)

Abaddon: Shall I keep going?
(Lori sits down slowly with a disturbing look. She stutters as she speaks.)
Lori: How how…how do you know all of this?
(Abaddon sits back and smile.)
Abaddon: I am Abaddon, a demon. I know everything.
Lori: Please! You work for some government or FBI.
Abaddon: Oh dear, ye hath little faith.

Know My Name

(Abaddon stares right into Lori eyes.)
Abaddon: You are a murder, and you will kill again soon.
Lori: What? I never killed anyone.
(Abaddon giggles.)
Abaddon: That's the beauty about you humans. You love to justify your action to make you feel good about yourself.
Lori: Yeah, I'm convinced that you are senile. You think I am someone in your past. Listen, I know some good doctors. Let Zack and I take you to the hospital.
Abaddon: Oh dear, you have killed twice and you will kill a

third time soon. Your recent victim, does he know about what you did.

(Lori doesn't have a clue as to what she is talking about.)

Lori: Who is he? Lady, you got the wrong person.

(Abaddon looks up. Her eyes roles halfway to the back. She raises her hands up as if she is about to do worship.)

Abaddon: Yes! Yes! The cries and ripping apart. We dance to the torture and pain. The sacrifices of babies practiced by the Levant region in the early Bronze Ages of a bullish head with a child burning in his belly…Topheth is Moloch, made of brass; and they heated him from his lower parts; and his hands being stretched out, and made hot, they put the children between his hands. The babies would scream and roll off into the fire. The babies would cry out; but the priests beat a drum, that the father might not hear the voice of his son.

(Abaddon eyes rolls back and put her hands down.)

Abaddon: God loves the children and the people he loves; loves hurting him by killing their own flesh and blood. Every century has its own godly or cult reason for sacrificing babies. Their reason was the gold bull Moloch to help bring rain and crops. Now, this century it is the worship of self.

Lori: What does this story have to do with me? Why are you telling me this.

Abaddon: Look who playing games now. Does David know what you did?

(Lori is baffled by what she is hearing. How does this person know so much about me? How does she know about what I did. No one knows about what she did.)

Lori: It wasn't murder!

(Abaddon laughs.)

Abaddon: That's right it wasn't alive at all. You know we have to hand it to you humans. Your species always come up with clever reasons to justify your evilness. Why didn't you tell David? I mean David is a good man. He really loved you.

(Lori is still quiet. Abaddon is starting to get to her.)

Lori: It is my body. He does not get a choice on the matter.

Abaddon: Ooh, selfish. I like it.

(Abaddon goggles.)

Abaddon: I bet he would have made a great father.

(Lori starts to tear up off that statement. Deep in her heart Abaddon is right. Lori gets angry.)

Lori: Shut up! I had enough of this. Open this door now or else.

(Abaddon looks over at the clock and looks back at Lori.)

Abaddon: It's almost time.

Lori: Almost time for what?

(Abaddon quickly changes the subject to her dad.)

Abaddon: What about your father?

Lori: What about him?

Abaddon: Why did you kill him?

Lori: Abaddon, I don't know what it is you are trying to do, but you are about to cross the line.

Abaddon: But Lori, we are getting closer.

Lori: My father was ill and was dying.

Abaddon: Come on Lori. You don't have to lie to me. Your father had one million dollars, all which came to you once you pulled the plug.

(Lori screams at Abaddon.)

Lori: Lies! That is not why I pulled the plug.

Abaddon: You sat there for days wishing he would just die already so you don't have to keep taking care of him. The day you found out about the money; you immediately made the decision to take him off life support…See two murders.

Lori: Those can't be consider murders.

Abaddon: Why? Is it because men said so?

(Lori looks down at her hands.)

Lori: I did what was best for…

Abaddon: Best for who? Remember Lori you will kill again. But let's talk about why we have called for you. We want you to tell our story.

Lori: What story?

Abaddon: Our gospel.

Lori: Your gospel? Like the bible?

Abaddon: Yes, just like the bible.

Lori: Who would want to read your story.

Abaddon: Who you ask…everyone! Look around you humans are already living my gospel.

Lori: So, what you consider yourself as an evil Jesus?

(Abaddon cringe at the when Lori mention Jesus name.)

Abaddon: No! Not like him.

(Abaddon looks around while talking.)

Abaddon: We just knew that we ripped God's heart out when Jesus fell to us. The goal was to have men turn his back against the so-called prophet. The world was ours and the Kingdom of God was ours. See, we don't care nothing for you humans. We just want to hurt God. Boy, were we wrong! The whole time this was in his plan the whole time. Jesus broke from the chains and gave us hell. We lost again...we were destroyed, lost in darkness. Yet, men would give us hope again. God made you in his image. He loves you more than anything. We could not understand why he loves you so much. Every day people rip his heart out and we rejoice. Every day you turn your back on him. You have a thought, and we just give you confirmation to go through with it...You blame him for all your problems. You justify immorality just to feel good about yourself. You worship self and curse God every chance you get. We offer the so-called sin, but you are the one who takes it.

(Abaddon leans in towards Lori.)

Abaddon: You are already living my gospel.

(Lori looks to the side.)

Lori: No, I will not be a part of this.

(Lori jumps up in anger.)

Lori: I'm getting the hell out of here. You can rot in hell!

(Lori grabs the chair and runs over to the living room window next to the front door. She takes a hard swing at the window and the chair breaks, but not the glass. She then grabs the nightstand and tries to break the window. Still nothing. Lori runs back to the dining room. To her surprise Abaddon is gone. Lori calls out for her.)

Lori: Abaddon! Where are you? Abaddon!

(Unknowingly, Abaddon is crawling on the ceiling above her a few feet back smile with glowing eyes. Lori walks back to the living room looking around. She hears a noise coming from upstairs.)

Lori: Abaddon, where are you?

(She reaches down and picks up one of the legs from the broken chair. Lori begins to walk up the stairs. While walking upstairs, Abaddon is crawling on the ceiling above her. Lori is unaware. Lori reaches the top of the stairs. She slowly opens the first bedroom door to the right of her.)

Lori: Abaddon, where are you? Come out now!

(Footsteps sound comes from the other room across. Lori pauses and then proceeds towards the other bedroom. She reaches for the doorknob and quickly opens the door. No one is in there. Running footsteps and giggles are behind Lori. She quickly turns around and nothing is there. Lori goes back into the hallway and looks around.)

Abaddon: Enough of the damn games! Let me out of here now!

(Lights go out and then comes back on. Abaddon is right in front of her as soon as the lights come on. Abaddon grabs her and rushes Lori against the wall. Lori screams.)

Abaddon: It's time Lori. It's time!

(Abaddon laughs and growls while attacking Lori. Lori fights back.)

Lori: Get the hell off of me!

(Lori pushes Abaddon back and takes a swing at Abaddon, striking her in the head. Abaddon falls down, Lori jumps over her and runs down the stairs. Abaddon herself up, both hands and feet on the ground. Abaddon crawls with her stomach facing up. She crawls after Lori.)

Abaddon: Its time Lori. It's time. Do not run, for it is now your destiny.

(Lori runs to the kitchen, grabs her phone. She runs to the basement to hide. She quietly hides behind some shovels kneel down and cover her mouth and nose. Abaddon is now standing at the top of the basement stairs. She slowly walks down the stairs.)

Abaddon: Oh Lori, come out sweat heart. There is nothing to be afraid of.

(Abaddon reaches the bottom of the stairs. Breathing heavy and looking around. Lori is doing her best to breathe quietly. A creepy demonic voice Abaddon calls for Lori again.)

Abaddon: Lori, come to me.

(Lori sees Abaddon from behind the shovel looking for her. Suddenly, Lori feels breathing behind her. Her eyes widen and fear comes over her. Lori turns around and Abaddon is right there pale with that creepy death smile and glowing eyes. Lori screams and Abaddon grabs her again.)

Lori: Let me go witch!

(Abaddon laughs and growls as she is attacking Lori.)

Abaddon: Time to give yourself to us.

(Lori manages to break free by kicking Abaddon off of her. She runs up the stairs through the kitchen into the dining room. Lori stops suddenly. Abaddon is standing right there. Lori backs up into the kitchen as Abaddon is approaching her.)

Lori: Get back now! Get. Back!

(Abaddon gets closer and closer. Lori backs up against the kitchen table.)

Abaddon: It's time now Lori.

(Abaddon launches at Lori. Lori falls down, Abaddon is choking her. Lori breaks out of her grip, knocks Abaddon to the side. Lori gets on top of her and uses the chair leg to choke Abaddon.)

Abaddon: Yes, that's it Lori…Yes.

(Lori pressed down harder with chair leg against Abaddon's neck until Abaddon is no longer breathing. Seconds passed. Lori gets off of her shaking and then she screams out. Breathing hard and disoriented from everything that has taking place. Lori slowly gets up. Abaddon is laying there dead. Tears ran down Lori's face. She wipes her face and walks quickly to the front door. As she reaches for the doorknob, the door opens, and Zack is right there with the intubation. Lori has so many emotions once she sees Zack.)

Zack: Man, took me a second but I found it.

(Lori pushes Zack angry.)

Lori: Where the hell were you! I called for you many times for help!

(Zack looks confused.)

Zack: What do you mean? I did not hear you. What's going on?

Lori: I've been stuck in this house for over an hour. What were you doing out there?

(Lori is screaming at him.)

Zack: Lori, I don't know what is going on or what you are

talking about. I was only gone for two minutes. Now, if you are done with the games I would like to get this lady some help.

Lori: Two minutes?

Zack: Yes, Lori…Look at you watch or phone.

(Lori looks at her watch and phone. Time is 12am. She cannot believe her eyes.)

Lori: two minutes? This can't be right.

Zack: Lori, I don't know what is going on with you, but we have to take care of this lady.

(Zack moves past Lori and heads to the kitchen. Lori is still trying to make sense of everything. She follows Zack to the kitchen and Abaddon is laid out the same way she was before Zack left out two minutes ago for the intubation. Zack feels for her pulse.)

Zack: She gone. Lori, when did she stop breathing?

(Lori is just staring.)

Zack: Lori! When did she stop breathing?

(Lori snaps out of it.)

Lori: I'm not sure.

(Zack calls in for more help.)

(A second ambulance arrives to help with the body. While Zack is talking to the other paramedics, Lori is sitting on the step in back of the ambulance still trying to make sense of what happened. Was this a dream, she thought to herself. She feels a push from behind, looks around and see nothing behind her. All of a sudden, a voice speaks out. The voice of Abaddon. Lori jumps up and looks around.)

Abaddon: Now, we are one Lori…Now we are one.

Lori: No, this cannot be!

Abaddon: You let us in.

Lori: No! Shut up! Stop!

(Zack and the other paramedics rush over to see what is going on.)

Zack: Lori! What are you doing?

Lori: It's in my head!

Zack: Who's in your head?

(Abaddon forces Lori to grab a scalpel.)

Zack: Lori, what are you doing with that scalpel?

Lori: It's not me! She's controlling me.

(Abaddon slowly forces Lori to take the scalpel and cut her own neck.)

Zack: Lori! Stop!

(Lori slits her throat. Zack screams. Lori grabs her throat with both hands. The other two paramedics rushed over and grabbed her. They moved her hands and to their surprise Lori throat was not cut. Not even a scratch. Lori cries out repeatedly.)

Lori: She's in my head! She's in my head!

The Book

(One year later, Lori is being interviewed at a popular syndicated radio station. The interviewer is asking Lori questions about the book she wrote and published.)

Radio Host: This is a compelling story. All this really happened.

Lori: Unfortunately, yes.

Radio Host: So, are you a believer now? Do you believe in a higher power?

(Lori hesitates to give it some thought before she answers.)

Lori: Yes, I guess I do believe in a higher power now. I'm sorry I don't guess…I'm sure of it.

Radio Host: This book here, is it the devil's bible.

Lori: No, I wrote this book as a warning.

Radio Host: A warning from what?

Lori: A warning on what's to come if we don't get right with God.

Radio Host: Awesome. Thank you, Lori, for coming on and sharing with us your story and your new book.

Lori: Thank you for having me.

Radio Host: My pleasure.

(Radio host ends the interview.)

Radio Host: Thank you for tuning in to 1200 PJT and make sure you pick up a copy of Lori's book.

(Lori gets up and says thank you again to the radio host and everyone else behind the scenes. She heads out of the station. As Lori is walking out to the parking lot a middle-aged man opens the door for her.)

Lori: Thank you sir.

Middle-aged man: You're welcome, Lori…Did you miss me? We miss you.

(Lori immediately stops. Her eyes get wide. The voice she hears is the voice of Abaddon. Lori turns around and the man is standing there with that same creepy pale smile. She is at a loss for words.)

Middle-aged man: You have some unfinished business.

(Fear comes over Lori as the middle-aged man laughs.)

Story Never Ends

(The stories are finished. Silence filled the basement. India looks to her right and left and see both Jacob and Larry are in a trance. She looks forward and the old man is gone. India tries to snap Larry and Jacob out of their trance by nudging them.)

India: Larry! Jacob! What's wrong with you two? Snap out of it!

(India shakes Jacob first and still nothing. She then slaps him. Jacob snaps out of his trance.)

Jacob: What the hell India!

(Jacob rubs the side of his face. India slaps Larry too. He snaps out of it as well.)

Larry: Damn India! What was that for?

India: You both were in deep trance.

(They get up and Jacob notice the old man is gone.)

Jacob: Where is the old man?

India: I don't know. As I was checking on you two and then looked up, he was gone.

(Larry ran over to the stairs.)

Larry: Guy's the door is open.

(Larry and India runs over to the stairs.)

Jacob: It is open. But where is the old man?

Larry: Who cares! Let's get out of here. We can call the cops once we get to the van and drive off.

(They run upstairs and rush to the front door. Jacob opens the door and they immediately run out. Something is not right. Once they ran through the door, they are back in the house.)

Larry: What the hell!

India: No! No, this is not real. Are we still sleeping?

Larry: How are we back in the house?

(Larry and India are freaking out. Jacob is doesn't know what to say.)

Larry: Jacob! Don't just stand there!

(Jacob snaps out of it.)

Jacob: I don't understand.

India: You don't understand what? How I told you, it was not a good idea to let that creep tell us those stupid stories.

Jacob: How is this my fault?

(Larry is talking to himself with India and Jacob is arguing. He's trying to rationalize what just happened.)

India: Are you kidding me?

(Larry turns to Jacob. He rushes Jacob against the door screaming at him.)

Larry: How is it your fault? You are the idiot who to this job!

(Jacob pushes Larry off of him.)

Jacob: Let me go!

(Jacob and Larry tussle. The door opens and they fall through. India is screaming telling them to stop.)

India: Would ya'll stop! Stop it!

(India tries to pull them apart. Larry swings at Jacob. Jacob leans back as Larry swings and ends up hit India in the face.)

India: Damnit!

(India holds the side of her face. Larry and Jacob stop and console India.)

Jacob: Larry, look at what you did!

Larry: Jacob, shut up…India, are you okay? I sorry.

(Larry reach for India but she pulls away.)

India: Move! You both are acting like idiots! We are in a damn haunted house and ya'll want to fight. Look around! We went through the front door twice and ended up back in the house. Jacob was there any other information about this house.

Jacob: No, nothing. Mr. Wright said the house has been abandoned for years.

Larry: We must be sleep or something. Maybe we have passed out from a gas leak.

India: How do you explain us sharing the same nightmare?

Larry: I don't know!

India: Well, we are definitely not sleep. You punch the crap out of me. I felt all of that.

(Larry looks down in shame.)

Larry: I'm sorry.

Jacob: Okay, we need to come up with a plan. You know what? We need to find that old creep and force him to get us out of here.

Larry: Find him? Um…have you notice this fool disappeared.

Jacob: He is here I know it. We just must look for him.

Larry: Jacob, don't you dare mention splitting up!

(Suddenly, they hear a knock at the door. They pause, staring at the door. Another knock and another knock. They look at each other with fear.)

Larry: Should we open it?

India: No! We don't know who's on the other side of that door.

Jacob: It could be someone here to help.

India: Oh yeah, suddenly everything is back to normal, and we can just walk out.

(A voice comes from the other side of the door.)

Voice: Hello? Is anyone home?

(Larry steps back from the door. They are confused about what they should do.)

Larry: Should I answer it now?

India: Why would someone come to an abandoned house?

Jacob: India is right, this could be another trap?

Larry: Another trap? What was the first one? Oh, that's right! You signed us up for this stupid job.

Voice: Hello? I heard noises, does anyone need some help?

(Larry goes back to the door.)

India: Larry what are you doing?

Jacob: Larry, don't answer the door!

(Larry reaches for the doorknob.)

Larry: He can help us get out of here.

Jacob: Get back now!

India: What the hell Larry! Stop!

(Larry turns the knob. As soon as he slightly opens the door, the door flies wide open knocking Larry back to the ground. Jacob and India help Larry up and what they see standing there is unimageable. Standing there is an eight-foot-tall pale human-like creature. With long stringy hair. Black eyes, long sharp teeth, and long arms to the knees. Fingernails are about three inches long. Skin is white like glue. The creature roars. India screams as she grips Larry's arm. Behind the human-like creature it is nothing but darkness. The creature speaks and sounds just like the old creepy man.)

Creature: It is time for your story to end.

(It approaches them and tries to grab Jacob. Jacob manages to avoid being grabbed.)

Jacob: Run!

(They all run towards the stairs leaning up. As they are running up the stairs, India looks back and sees the creature coming after them. At the top of the stairs Jacob guides everyone down the long hallway to the last room. Once they enter the room Jacob quickly and quietly closes the door before the creature sees them. The last room is large with many places to hide. India and Jacob hides in the closet. Larry hides underneath a large desk. India whisper to Jacob.)

India: Jacob, what was that?

Jacob: I think that is the old man.

India: How could that be? Where are we?

Jacob: I am not sure, but we have to get out of here.

(India beings to cry. Jacob tries to calm her down.)

India: It won't let us leave. There is no way out.

Jacob: There is away…I know it. We just have to figure it out.

India: Jacob…I don't want to die.

Jacob: You won't die.

(They hear the footsteps of the creature coming down the hallway.)

Creature: Don't be scared…Come, let me tell you another story.

(The door to the room opens. Larry peaks around the desk and sees the creature standing in the doorway. The creature smells the air.)

Creature: I can taste your fear.

(The creature laughs. The creature looks right in the direction where Larry is. Larry moves back and covers his mouth, hoping the creature did not see him. The creature comes in fully knocking things over in search of them. India covers her mouth, so she does not make noise. Jacob has the closet door crack just enough to see what the creature is doing.)

Creature: Come out come out. There's no need to be afraid.

We will become one.

(Creature laughs.)

Creature: Don't you want to know how your story will end?

(The creature is now over the desk where Larry is hiding. He flips the desk over, but Larry is gone. Larry crawled behind some large boxes. The creature roars in frustration. It leaves out the room.)

Jacob: The creature is gone, but I don't see Larry. India, stop breathing so hard.

India: I'm not breathing hard.

(Jacob turn around slowly to India. His eyes get wide. Jacob can barely speak. India eyes gets wide, and fear comes over her face. She feels the breath of the creature on the back of her neck. The creature is behind her. She whispers to Jacob with tears running down her face.)

India: Jacob…

(Jacob quickly opens the closet door and grabs India.)

Jacob: Run!

(They rush out of the closet, but the creature India by the leg. India screams and Jacob is trying to pull her from the creature. It bites her leg, and she screams again. Larry runs over and helps Jacob pull India out. Larry sees a glass vase; he breaks it and grabs a sharp piece of glass. Larry stabs the creature multiple times in the hand and arm. The creature finally let go of India. Jacob slams the door; Larry pushes the dresser in front of the door. They help India up and run out of the room. India can barely keep up due to the wound on her leg.)

Jacob: Let go! This way.

India: I can't. My leg.

(Larry and Jacob helps India down the stairs. They carry her down another hallway and stop at the second room. Jacob closes the door. They put India on the bed. Jacob and Larry push a dresser in front of the door.)

Jacob: Larry, check the closet!

(Larry opens the closet door. He breaks the door so this time the creature will not sneak up on them. Jacob takes a look at India's leg. Her leg looks like a medium shark bit her leg. There is green liquid oozing out of her leg. Jacob looks worried.)

India: How does my leg look?

Jacob: It looks just fine.

(Jacob pulls Larry to the side.)

Jacob: Larry, her leg looks bad man.

Larry: What should we do? There is no way out and this thing won't stop.

Jacob: I will lure the creature out. Once I do this, you and India must find a way out.

Larry: What about you?

Jacob: I'll be behind ya'll.

Larry: Man! That's a stupid idea.

Jacob: Maybe, but it is the only way to get free from here.

(India cries out in agony. Jacob and Larry look back at her.)

Jacob: Larry, you must make sure she gets out of here. While this thing is focused on me, whatever power it has over this house should break, allowing you both to run out the front door.

Larry: You need a weapon to protect yourself.

(Jacob and Larry look around the room to find a weapon for Jacob. Jacob sees in the corner of the room a long metal pole. He goes over and picks up the metal pole and feels the weight of it. Jacob looks over to Larry and smiles.)

Jacob: This should do.

(Jacob walks over to the door and cracks it open slightly enough to see down the hall.)

Jacob: Okay, remember as soon as you get the chance, get India out of here.

Larry: How will we know when to leave?

Jacob: You will know.

(Jacob closes the door and takes a deep breath. He then opens the door again and slowly steps out. There are long cracks on the hallway walls. Wind whispers up and down the hall. Jacob turns back to Larry and India and gives them a nod. He closes the door behind him. Jacob can hear his own heartbeat as he begins to walk. He calls out for the creature.)

Jacob: Where are you…you creepy bastard!

(Jacob hits both sides of the walls with the metal pole for the creature to come.)

Jacob: Come on! Show me how my story will end.

(Larry peeks to see what is going on.)

India: Do you see him?

Larry: No. Not anymore. I do hear him.

(Jacob has now entered the living room. Each step he takes the floor creaks. He feels something is watching him. A gust of wind blows past him. Jacob quickly turns around and sees nothing.)

Jacob: Enough with the games! Come get me!

(Loud running footsteps come up behind Jacob. He turns and swings the pole at the same time, but nothing was there. More loud running behind him, Jacob swings again. Still nothing. Suddenly, Jacob is slapped on the side of his head by the creature. He flies across the room landing on and breaking. Jacob also drops the pole. He sees it and crawls over quickly to get to the pole. The creature follows over and steps on the pole as Jacob tries to pick it up. It grabs Jacob and throws him against the wall. Jacob looks over and next to him are two pencils. The creature grabs him again and lifts him up. It opens its mouth wide. Jacob stabs it in the right eye. It roars out a loud scream, dropping Jacob. Jacob runs over to the metal pole and picks it up. This time Jacob swings, striking the creature in the head knocking it down.)

Larry: India, that's our signal!

(Larry helps India up. They get to the door.)

Larry: You ready?

India: Ready as I will ever be.

(They hear Jacob fighting with the creature. Larry and India run out of the room and down the hall. India falls.)

India: Larry!

(Larry turns back to help India. The creature hears them trying to escape. It tries to go after them, but Jacob stabs it on the side of its ribs with the pole. It roars loud and turns to Jacob knocking him in the kitchen. Jacob yells out to Larry and India.)

Jacob: Run! Get out of here!

(Larry and India makes it to the front door. Larry hears Jacob's fighting with the creature. He looks back. India opens the door. She sees the van.)

India: Larry, we must go! Jacob will make it.

(They both rush out towards the van. Jacob picks up a chair and slams it against the creature body. One of the legs broke off in the shape of a wooden steak. Larry and India are now in the van. Larry starts the van.)

Larry: Come on Jacob. Come on man…You can make it.

India: You think he's …

Larry: Don't say it! Jacob is coming.

(Jacob picks up the wooden steak. The creature comes up behind him and bites Jacob on the left shoulder. Jacob screams out. The creature bites down even harder. Jacob takes the steak and stabs it in the side of its face. The creature let go immediately. Jacob turns around and pulls the steak out and stabs it again in the chest, it falls. Jacob runs to the front door. At that moment Jacob runs out and the creature grabs his leg pulling him back into the house. Jacob grabs the door border with both hands, trying to break free.)

Creature: Your story ended with me feasting on you!

(Jacob is handing on for his life. He is losing grip. The more it pulls the weaker Jacob gets. Jacob and no longer hanging on. He let go and Larry is right there. He quickly grabs both of Jacob hands. Jacob looks at Larry with a sigh of relief. It is tug of war between Larry and the creature.)

Larry: Our story does not end here! Let go bastard!

(Larry pulls and pulls. Jacob is in agony from being pulled in different directions.)

Jacob: Larry, let me go. Save yourself.

Larry: No! Don't dare give up!

(India grabs a long screwdriver. She gets out of the car and runs over as fast as she can. India stabs the creature multiple times until it let go. It let go of Jacob. Larry and falls back off the porch with Jacob. India jumps down and fall because of her leg. They all got up and ran to the van. The door slams shut. Larry quickly pulls off. They drove about a mile away. Larry pulls over.)

India: Why are you stopping?

Larry: What do we do now?

(Jacob looks out the window.)

Jacob: I don't know…No one will believe what happened to

us.

Larry: They have too…Like, look at you two wounds.

(Jacob grabs his shoulder.)

Larry: Damn man, we were in a real-life horror movie.

(They all laugh. Larry beings driving again. It is now ten o'clock pm. They have arrived back to the office. They get out of the van and slowly walk in. The office is empty.)

Larry: Hey guys, I'm going to get my stuff and leave…I think I quit.

India: Larry, that's the best thing you said all day. I quit too.

(They laugh.)

Jacob: I going to lock up and leave the keys and a note. I'm sure there will be a lot of questions come Monday.

(Larry heads to the bathroom. He looks in the mirror and washes his face. Larry shakes his head and walks out.)

Larry: Hey guys, maybe we can write a book about this.

(Larry jokingly says.)

Larry: We can at least get some money off this. What ya'll think?

(It is quiet and dark. Larry does not hear Jacob or India.)

Larry: Hey! Did ya'll leave? Jacob? India?

(No one answered.)

Larry: Hello!

(Larry is looking around.)

Larry: I know ya'll not trying to play games…especially, after what we just went through.

(Larry is walking through the office. Behind him India appears.)

India: This is how our story ends.

(Larry turns around and sees India. Her eyes are black like the old man and creature. Larry is confused.)

Larry: India, stop playing.

(She starts walking toward Larry.)

India: This is how our story ends.

Larry: Ha! Funny, let's go. Where is Jacob.

(Jacob appears behind Larry.)

Larry: This is how our story ends.

(Larry turns around quickly and sees Jacob. Jacob eyes are black just like India's eyes.)

Larry: What the hell! Jacob!
(Jacob also starts walking towards Larry.)
Jacob: This is how our story ends.
(Both Jacob and India are repeating this multiple times as they approach Larry. Larry takes steps back and they move closer.)
Larry: What happened? You both have the same dark eyes.
(Larry runs from both, towards the door. Jacob and India chase after him. Larry runs out and closes the door, locking them inside. Larry runs and gets in his car. He pulls off immediately)
Larry: What the hell happened to them?
(Larry thinks to himself.)
Larry: Their bites. It was their bites.
(Two voices appeared in his car within him. He looks through his rearview mirror and sees Jacob in the back and India is sitting next to him.)
Jacob and India: This is how our story ends.
Larry: How the…
(Jacob and India attacks Larry. Screams echo the streets from the car.)
(At the house the old creepy man is in the basement. He puts a photo of Jacob, India, and Larry. He smiles.)
Old Creepy Man: This is how all stories ends.
(Laughter echoes throughout the house.)

This is how all stories end.
This is how all stories end.
This is how all stories end.

www.ingramcontent.com/pod-product-compliance
Lightning Source LLC
LaVergne TN
LVHW091036150826
845672LV00006BA/1837

9798891845237